W9-BMY-163

THE ROGUE'S SEDUCTION

LAUREN SMITH

Lauren Smith

This book is a work of fiction. Names, characters, places, and incidents are the product of the author's imagination or are used fictitiously. Any resemblance to actual events, locales, or persons, living or dead, is coincidental.

Copyright © 2017 by Lauren Smith

Edited by Noah Chinn

Excerpt from *The Duelist's Seduction* by Lauren Smith

Cover art by Erin Dameron Hill

Romance Art by Theresa Sprekelmeyer

All rights reserved. In accordance with the U.S. Copyright Act of 1976, the scanning, uploading, and electronic sharing of any part of this book without the permission of the publisher constitutes unlawful piracy and theft of the author's intellectual property. If you would like to use material from the book (other than for review purposes), prior written permission must be obtained by contacting the publisher at lauren@laurensmithbooks.com. Thank you for your support of the author's rights.

The publisher is not responsible for websites (or their content) that are not owned by the publisher.

ISBN: 978-1-947206-02-1 (e-book edition)

ISBN: 978-1-947206-03-8 (print edition)

OTHER TITLES BY LAUREN SMITH

Contemporary
The Surrender Series
The Gilded Cuff
The Gilded Cage
The Gilded Chain
Her British Stepbrother
Forbidden: Her British Stepbrother
Seduction: Her British Stepbrother
Climax: Her British Stepbrother

Paranormal
Dark Seductions Series
The Shadows of Stormclyffe Hall
The Love Bites Series
The Bite of Winter
Brotherhood of the Blood Moon Series
Blood Moon on the Rise
Brothers of Ash and Fire
Grigori
Mikhail
Rurik

Sci-Fi Romance
Cyborg Genesis Series
Across the Stars (coming soon)

For my grandmother, Rhea, who always had a secret stash of bodice rippers for me to read.

CHAPTER 1

London, December 1821

L   Perdita Darby tugged the hood of her cloak close about her face, shielding herself not just from the bitter wind that battered the hackney coach she'd hired, but from any watchful eyes lurking in the shadows. The street was empty, twilight and the cold having chased even the most dedicated late-night strollers to their homes. Even the street urchins, usually desperate for coin, were tucked away in their alleyways on a bitingly cold night such as this, seeking what warmth they could. Perdita feared the darkness might hide someone who would realize who she was or what she was going to do. That could spell ruin.

"M'lady?" The driver of the hired coach stood by the door and closed it as she tugged her skirts free. He began to doff his cap at her, but she waved for him to keep it on. The night was too cold for such things. He smiled gratefully and kicked the snow off his boots.

"Please wait for me here." She pressed a few coins in his palm, and he nodded.

"Of course." The driver pocketed the coins and climbed back

up onto his seat. He bundled his heavy brown cloak over his body and huddled down for warmth.

Perdita faced the door of the townhouse in front of her. It was a lovely home, one that had been on Duke Street for many years. The noble arches were framed with ivy that grew up from the flower beds bordering the windows, even though the leaves had dropped away to expose the skeletal webbing of vines beneath. But in spring when the ivy was bright and sprawling, it would make this house look almost like a cottage deep in the Cotswolds, not a stately townhouse in the midst of a bustling city.

It was clear the owner of this house didn't bother with a gardener who would have kept the ivy from spreading. But that shouldn't have surprised her. She knew the owner of this house. Perdita planned to throw herself at his feet and beg for his help if she had to, and it didn't matter if ballroom whispers called him the Devil of London.

She squared her shoulders.

Be brave. He's the only one who can help you. Don't let him know how frightened you are.

She marched up the steps and rapped the metal knocker mounted on the stout oak door. Suddenly doubt assailed her. This was a terrible idea. Her mind screamed at her to flee as she stood upon the threshold to the underworld.

Perhaps she could beg her parents to let her go to the continent for a few years and avoid the fate that had driven her to this door at such an hour. Yet that would only spare her, not her family, of the consequences of running away from the blackmail she was facing.

The door creaked, the old oak protesting as the hinges grudgingly gave in. A middle-aged butler stood there, his beady eyes peering down at her over his long, thin nose and pointed chin. His professional demeanor lacked the politeness expected of a servant in a decent household. His shoulders were broad, and he seemed far too muscular for a refined position of a butler. But this wasn't a decent household. This was the devil's own home.

"Er..." He blinked at her, apparently startled by her appearance. It was a risk to be seen standing on this particular doorstep after midnight, a fact of which she was all too aware.

"I must see Lord Darlington at once," she told the man, praying he would let her inside. She could not take the risk of being seen and starting a scandal. Or rather, a different scandal than the one she was meticulously planning already.

The man hesitated, his body barring her entrance through the still partially closed door. "This is late, even for my master."

Perdita didn't back down. "I am aware of the hour, but he will want to see me." She raised her chin and announced this with such regal bearing that he would not dare question her. He sighed and stepped away from the doorway. Her mother's lessons, it seemed, hadn't been wasted on her after all.

"This way, madam." He waved a hand for her to step inside. She entered the townhouse, her body relaxing, but only just. She may have been out of view of the street, but she was still in very dangerous territory.

Two dim lamps illuminated the hall and staircase. She was surprised they were still lit. Was the master of the house still awake? She had assumed he would be, but the house was hushed and ghostly quiet. She took a moment to study her surroundings with open curiosity. The foyer was bare of any decorations, paintings, or even end tables. The starkness of it surprised her.

So this is where the Devil of London resides.

The furniture she glimpsed through a cracked-open door a few feet away—the drawing room perhaps—was outdated and threadbare. It made sense. The master of this house was rumored to be a desperate fortune hunter in dire straits. His desperation was no fault of his own, but rather due to his parents' untimely deaths and their accumulated debts.

It had to be a heavy burden to enter adulthood with the responsibilities of maintaining title and lands held in one's own family without any money by which to do so. Any man in such a position was a *dangerous* man—particularly when it came to rich, unmarried heiresses.

Like me...

"Please wait while I speak to the master. Who shall I say is calling?" the butler asked.

"Perdita Darby," she said, trying to still her trembling as she watched the butler go upstairs.

Perdita swallowed the knot of fear in her throat. This man had been desperate enough to kidnap her dearest friend, Alexandra Rockford, in order to win a five-thousand-pound wager by seducing her. That alone earned him his nickname in her eyes. To treat a woman's virtue as something to be wagered on! In the end, however, he had failed. Alexandra had been rescued by Ambrose Worthing, a man so in love with her he had fought his best friend to free her.

Alexandra had assured Perdita that Lord Darlington hadn't been *entirely* wicked—he'd only planned to convince the men involved in the wager that he had bedded her when he had not. But that did not make the Devil of London a hero, by any means. At best, he was a villain with a conscience. But Perdita was desperate enough to risk herself in his house tonight, knowing the danger and scandal that could fall upon her.

This is a terrible idea. Unfortunately, she had no other option. Only Lord Darlington could help her. She was prepared to do just about anything to escape her situation.

"Madam." The butler appeared at the top of the stairs. "His Lordship will see you now."

Perdita stared up at him, startled. "Upstairs? Not the drawing room?"

The old codger had the audacity to grin at her. "He insisted you meet upstairs, or I was to show you out."

The nerve of the man, demanding she meet him upstairs! Did he treat all gentle-bred ladies like this? Or, knowing who was paying a call upon him, he was perhaps doing his best to frighten her off. Yes, that must be it. He thought she would be too afraid to go upstairs.

I'm not afraid. Well, I am, but I'll be damned if I let him know that.

She lifted her skirts and ascended the stairs, her heart hammering. She followed the butler to a room where the door was slightly ajar. She glanced at the servant, but he was already departing.

Perdita pushed the door open and froze when she realized it was a bedchamber. Darlington had the audacity to call her to his *bedchamber?* Did he believe she had come for amorous reasons, or that she would condone such a brazen attempt at seduction? It was entirely possible, given the scandalous hour and the fact she was without a chaperone, but she would set him straight if he dared to try to seduce her.

She wished for the hundredth time it would have been possible to visit him during the day, but there had been no alternative. People would have seen her enter his home, and that would be the end of her carefully kept reputation. She tensed when a dark, rich voice spoke.

Vaughn Darlington, the viscount dubbed by *ton* as the Devil of London. His voice sent tingles of excitement and fear through her. She took an instinctive step back toward the door.

"Fleeing so soon? I would have wagered you were braver than that, Miss Darby. Or perhaps, given the lateness of the hour and the method of this meeting, I should call you Perdita?"

She bristled and pushed the hood of her cloak back to better peer around the room. There was a four-poster bed against one wall and a fire crackling in the hearth. The wood floor showed dusty outlines of where carpets had recently been. The dark-green brocaded curtains about the bed were faded, and a few rings were missing, letting the fabric gape in odd places. Worn and peeling silk wallpapers depicting men hunting in the forest covered the walls. A once beautiful wardrobe stood in one corner, a door missing. The shaving stand held a white china basin with a large crack down its side.

The masculine air of the room was overpowering, just as the man himself was, but the circumstances and the condition of his rooms filled her with a strange pity that made her go still as she turned her focus on the man himself.

Leaning against one worn, ancient chair was Lord Darlington. He was tall, broad shouldered, and had a dangerous look about his all too beautiful face. With piercing blue eyes and light-blond hair, Darlington could have passed for an angel if it weren't for the sensual, wicked curve of his lips. He wore buff trousers and a white lawn shirt, with a dark-blue waistcoat. His cravat had been untied and lay loose over the back of one chair.

Perdita's heart quickened. She had never stood in a room with a man in a state of partial undress like this. She forced herself to rally to the task at hand.

"Lord Darlington, I come here with a proposal." Her tone was brusque with a manner of business about it. This was not about seduction, no matter how sinful he made her feel. Though she'd rehearsed this speech a dozen times on her own, she had not been prepared for the strange and frightening feelings that assaulted her now as she spoke to him alone.

He crossed his arms as he studied her with that wicked twist of his lips, making her breath quicken. She shifted in place, and her boots scraped softly against the wood floor.

"Do go on." He chuckled, seeming to enjoy her discomfort.

"Well, you see..." She spoke haltingly, still mortified that she was here begging him for his help. "I need to stop an unwanted marriage proposal." She twined her fingers nervously as she removed her gloves. "My mother has convinced a certain gentleman that I am willing to consider his offer, when I most certainly am not."

She tried not to think of Mr. Samuel Milburn and how that man had made it clear he would imprison her in a life that would slowly kill her. She could still see him leaning in close to her and whispering: *"The women I care for know better than to seek the company of others, when I should be enough. My home has all you will need, so I will hear no talk of travel or nights out. They would only distract you from your duty, which would be pleasing me."*

He was a brute and a tyrant and worse, but Perdita's mother, despite her ambitious nature, didn't usually believe in society gossip.

Perdita did. She'd heard that Milburn had thrown a woman to her death from a window, but because the woman was his mistress, no questions were asked. It had been dismissed as an unfortunate accident. All Perdita knew for sure was that this man was a monster. She had tried to tell her father and mother what she'd heard, but her words had been dismissed as idle talk. If her older brother Thomas hadn't been away at sea serving in His Majesty's royal navy, she would have sought his help.

In Perdita's experience, being a wealthy heiress was a terrible burden. It put a mark on her. She'd fought off fortune hunters for the last few years, but a man like Milburn was dangerous in other ways. He didn't care about her money—he cared about breaking her spirit and possibly even killing her if she didn't give him what he desired. She was *sport*.

She'd made the mistake of meeting him at a dinner party last fall, and he had immediately shown an interest in her once he'd learned she was none other than Miss Darby, the beloved lady of the *ton* who all sought to please with their praise and their many invitations.

Perdita had not wished to cultivate such a favored reputation on purpose, but it had happened quite naturally. But to Milburn she became a prize he wished to win—and then suffocate and destroy. Once he had her in his sights, he had been able to contrive a scheme that could destroy her family and blackmail her into accepting his proposal.

"What does this have to do with me? Or did you merely wish to tumble in my sheets to avoid marrying some silly young buck? I don't care much for ruining innocents, but in your case I might make an exception," Darlington said, his sharp gaze on her.

Perdita considered reminding him he had in fact attempted to ruin her innocent friend over a wager, but she thought better of it. Quarreling with him now would not aid her in acquiring his help.

"I wish to engage your services." She still couldn't say the words. It was too humiliating.

"My services?" He shifted slightly, a frown curving his lips. "What *services* do you require?" When Darlington said *services*, it sounded sinful, wicked.

"I wish to hire your cooperation in appearing to be engaged to me, publicly. Not a true engagement, just for a few months, to deter the other gentleman so he will leave me be." She glanced down, playing with her gloves. She was betting that Milburn would lose interest if he believed he had another challenger for her hand.

His eyes turned wintry, almost chilling as they settled on her fidgeting hands. "So I'm to play your fiancé? What's to be my reward in scaring the bounder off?" Darlington still leaned against the side of the chair, but Perdita was more aware of him than ever. The small distance between them seemed to shrink every second.

"I will pay you. I have access to some of my dowry. It is invested in a private bank with Lady Rosalind Lennox. My father put the funds in his name, but he allows me to have some control over them."

Darlington stroked his chin. "I require a more permanent solution than a temporary flow of money. You said you bank with Lady Lennox?" He continued to stare at her with that assessing gaze, and she suddenly feared he might not agree, that he might consider blackmailing her directly for her funds in the bank by exposing her visit to his townhouse. Surely he wouldn't dare.

When he still gazed at her expectantly, she realized he awaited some response to his question. She nodded.

"Then you are acquainted with Lord Lennox, her husband? He is a selective but successful investor. I wish to be involved in whatever scheme he chooses to invest in next."

Perdita nodded again. She was well acquainted with Rosalind Lennox, but she only knew of her husband, Ashton Lennox, in passing. Perhaps she could persuade Rosalind to allow Darlington to invest with her husband. She only hoped such a request wouldn't seem inappropriate to her friend. It was a risk she had to take to avoid marriage to a man like Samuel Milburn.

"I believe I can arrange a meeting. As to whether he allows you to invest..." There was no way she could guarantee that.

Darlington pushed away from the chair and came up to her. The simple action seemed to change everything between them. Before he hadn't seemed so threatening. But now with his towering frame so close, she felt very much like a tiny rabbit facing a very large wolf. She knew he was tall, but standing inches away from him made her feel small and feminine in a way she never had before. It took a moment for her to catch her breath. She had to tilt her face back to look up at him.

"I suppose that would be good enough. But you know once we have begun this charade, everyone will expect us to marry." It sounded like he was warning her. They would never marry. If there was one thing she was certain of, she would *not* marry the Devil of London.

"I am aware of that. After a time I deem prudent, you may cry off our engagement and go on as you please." She had to be completely sure Samuel Milburn was no longer interested in her, and only then could she risk a public break with Lord Darlington. Otherwise, her family's reputation would be ruined, and her father might be facing penalties under English law.

His lips twitched in an amused smile. "And you are ready to

brave the *ton* after being jilted by me?" The wolfish smile that stole across his lips was not reassuring. "I doubt any other man would have you once I've been your lover."

"We would not be lovers, only engaged."

Darlington laughed softly. "Any woman I asked to marry me would certainly be my lover beforehand. I wouldn't wish to marry a woman unless I was positive I enjoyed my time with her in bed."

She ignored his scandalous words. "Being jilted by the likes of you, even if some assume we've been lovers, is better than having a man like Samuel Milburn find a way to compromise me. I know the sort of man he is, and as unbelievable as it is, he is *worse* than you." She threw her shoulders back and glared at him, daring him to argue the point.

"Milburn?" Darlington's eyes widened. "That's the man who is chasing your skirts?"

"Yes. Do you know him?"

He nodded slowly. "Unfortunately, I do. We've run into each other at various clubs." He paused as though choosing his words carefully, weighing what she ought to hear or not as the case might be. "Most of the *ton* see him as a delightful gentleman who could do no wrong. Others know him as I do. Some would say he and I have similar tastes in pain—not in receiving it but causing it."

"A taste for pain?" Perdita shuddered. She'd heard Milburn had thrown his mistress out of a window. Any future with a man like that would seal her fate, but she hadn't heard the same of Darlington. He wasn't cruel, though she'd heard he was impossibly *wicked*. Even a fleeting kiss upon the hand during an introduction had been known to cause such scandals that ladies in the ballroom took flight to escape, like a flock of birds dressed in silk and tulle.

"Yes." Darlington's eyes were on her face again. "We require something a little different in our bed play." He paused again, his eyes dark and fathomless as he stared at her. "But unlike him, my goal is *always* pleasure. A crying, hurting woman is not arousing to me. But for Milburn, it makes his blood turn to fire."

Darlington's bold words on such a subject made her take another step back.

"You like to cause *pain* in bed?" She hated how her words trembled as they escaped her. Surely whispers of this would have reached her if that were true. "This was a mistake. I should—"

He reached up and cupped her cheek when she tried to pull away, then wound a strong arm around her waist, her cloak bunching above her bottom. She had to face him now and hear whatever it was he wished to say.

"There are two types of pain, love. One is slight, expected, and leads to intense pleasure. The other is selfish and part of a need to be cruel and harsh. I prefer the former, not the latter."

His words didn't make any sense. Pain was pain, wasn't it? She wrinkled her nose and prepared to argue this, but she never had the chance. He lowered his head and captured her mouth with his. Perdita was frozen in shock. The feel of his soft warm lips moving over hers was strange but increasingly delightful.

She'd never been kissed before but had often imagined how it would feel. She mimicked his mouth and gasped as he licked the seam of her lips with his tongue. The velvety feel of his tongue touching her lips was both sinful and decadent. Her knees went weak beneath her heavy skirts. She grasped his shoulders, frantic not to lose hold of him. The heat between their mouths intensified, and a heady dazed feeling began to slink through her limbs and into her lower belly. She could do this for hours...

His lips wandered from hers down to her throat just above where her cloak covered her shoulders. He placed a kiss there and then suddenly nipped her skin with his teeth. The bite sent a jolt through her, and a fierce, shocking pulse beat between her thighs. She whimpered and tried to push away, not because it hurt, but because the rush of sensations had been too much. She'd never—

"That, my love, is pain mixed with pleasure." Darlington whispered this against the skin of her throat, still holding her fast so she could not escape. Shivers rippled down her spine, and she closed her eyes. This was frightening. *He* was frightening, but a part of her wanted to understand more of what he was showing her.

From the moment she'd first seen him at her mother's garden party a few months before, she'd been intrigued by his mysteries. She wouldn't deny it. Any decent young lady would not have allowed herself to be fascinated by such a notorious rogue, but now more than ever she wondered if perhaps she wasn't as decent as she ought to be.

Darlington slowly released her waist, but the hand that still held her face seemed to burn her skin. He brushed his thumb over her lips, leaving a tingling sensation that trailed from her mouth down to her toes. She raised her eyes to his, her world tilting on its axis as she stared up at him. There was no going back from that kiss. She'd taken a bite of the forbidden apple, and the juices were sweet upon her lips.

"You're still trembling," he observed, his voice was low and gentle, but rather than soothe her, she felt excited by it.

"It is always like that?" she asked, wondering why Mother had never mentioned that lips could meet in such a blaze of fire when she'd discussed the ways men and women could be together.

Darlington touched her lips once more before dropping his hands. "Not always. Too many marriages are built upon the wrong foundations, and passions are rarely taken into account." He turned away from her and walked over to the fire, placing one hand on the mantle as he gazed into the flames.

"If you want to play this game, Miss Darby, it must be played convincingly. Milburn won't accept a mere declaration of our engagement. He knows me too well. He's also not the sort to give up easily." Darlington's face was lit by firelight. For a moment, he looked more like Hades, the Greek god of the underworld, than a mere London rogue. Perdita was entranced by the sight of him. He was a lure she couldn't resist. How many women had come into his room before her and fallen under his spell?

"What did you have in mind?"

"I suppose you recall what befell Alexandra Rockford in my

home? A public display. *That* is what I mean. Milburn will need to see us in a compromising position." He turned to face her. "And that means more than a simple kiss."

Perdita bit her bottom lip. A simple kiss? Not to her. That kiss had been her undoing. She was wise enough to know he had changed her life in a few short minutes.

"If it helps me escape Samuel Milburn, then I agree to do whatever is necessary." She raised her chin, earning a slow smile from him that made her blush.

"What?" she demanded as he continued to smile at her.

"I never would've guessed you would agree. Of all ladies, you seem to be the most..."

Perdita narrowed her eyes. "Most what?"

"Let us say I'm surprised at your defiant streak, that is all."

Perdita stared at him challengingly. "I behave appropriately in public, a dutiful daughter and a well-bred lady, but you have no idea what sort of woman I really am." He truly didn't. She was a lady, well-versed in conversation, a charming hostess, a delight among the *ton*, but that wasn't all she was. There were other, hidden sides of herself she dared not reveal.

Darlington's eyes sparkled with mischief. "Now *that* is most interesting. As your fiancé, I will make it my sacred duty to uncover these hidden facets of your character."

She tilted her head, studying him in return. "How about your services then?" She wanted to keep this matter as businesslike between them as she could manage. He would no doubt rob her of her good sense with his kisses, but if she held fast and reminded them both this was only business and nothing more, then perhaps she might survive this devil's bargain with her heart intact.

"I have one last question before I agree, and I demand honesty in your answer."

She weighed the risk of losing his help against any question he might demand and then nodded. "Ask."

"What hold does Milburn have over you that leaves you in such fear? I do not believe for a moment that your parents would force you to accept a match with him even if he dragged you down with scandal. No, there is something that makes you fear you might have no choice to accept if he pursues you." Darlington played with the cuffs of his right-hand sleeve. "What does he hold over you, Miss Darby?"

It was the one question she didn't want to answer, but she knew she had to.

"In private, he has claimed that he can prove my father was involved in the smuggling of goods into England and evading taxes." She hesitated, hoping she could trust Darlington with such information.

"And is he? Guilty, I mean?"

"No! I mean, that is to say, *he* isn't. But I fear the men he invests with might very well be guilty. I believe Milburn might even be working with them to frame my father, and unfortunately I have no way of stopping them. If I marry him, he says he will destroy the evidence, but if I do not..."

"And you believe that an engagement to me will stop him?"

"It has to," she whispered. "If he no longer desires me, then he has no reason to go through with his threats. And you are one of the most wicked men in London. If he isn't afraid of you and tries to take what is yours, such as a future wife, he would be mad."

The corners of lips twitched. "That is certainly true. I wouldn't hesitate to destroy any who dared take what is mine, especially a woman. Very well, I agree to this scheme, mad though it is." Darlington held out one hand to her. "Shall we shake upon it?" He was quite serious, except for the wicked gleam in his eyes. A gleam that promised every moment with him would be deliciously sinful torture.

Perdita placed her palm in his. "We have an accord."

"Agreed." He turned her hand in his, lifting it to his lips as he kissed her knuckles.

"Good." She hesitated, relishing the feel of his lips upon her bare fingers before she tugged her hand free of his. "My mother is hosting a Christmas party at our estate in Lothbrook. I will see to it that you are invited. Please bring your valet, and have him pack enough clothes to last through Christmas."

Darlington nodded, but when she turned to leave, he caught her arm.

"Yes? Lord Darlington?" She eyed his hand on her arm. He did not release her, not like another man would.

"Given our new intimacy, it would please me to be called Vaughn whenever we are alone."

"Vaughn." She tested the sound of his given name, hating that she liked how smoothly it rolled off her tongue.

"And I expect to be introduced to Lord and Lady Lennox before the end of this year. Will that be possible?"

Perdita nodded. "Yes. I will arrange it as soon as I can."

"Good." He tucked her arm in his. "Let me escort you out."

"Really, my lord—Vaughn. There's no need."

"I need to practice playing the part of a gentleman. I fear I may be a bit rusty."

She remained silent as he led her down the stairs. When he opened the front door, she paused as the bitter wind cut through her. She glanced at him a moment longer before she pulled her cloak hood back up, concealing her features. She rushed to the waiting coach and climbed inside. She chanced one last peek at him through the curtains. He stood there in the doorway without a coat. She remembered the heat of his body pressed to hers and shivered, but not from the cold.

How strange to have made a bargain with Vaughn, Viscount Darlington. They were now bound together, and though they were united in their mission, she felt incredibly alone. She wished she could talk to her dear friend Alexandra, but she was the last person Perdita could confide in when it came to Vaughn.

When Vaughn had kidnapped Alex, it had been a terrifying ordeal, even after Vaughn had revealed he had no intention of harming her. When Alex learned of her supposed engagement to Vaughn, she would no doubt rush to Perdita and try to put a stop to her madness. It was not a meeting Perdita looked forward to, but she and Alex had such different views on how to handle society. Alex had hidden from it while Perdita had embraced it.

Perdita needed Vaughn's dangerous reputation. It was the last shield she had against Samuel Milburn. It was something her dear friend would not understand because she was not the target of Milburn's evil intent. Perdita had sold her soul to a lesser devil to protect herself from a worse one.

She prayed only that their scheme would work, or she was doomed.

CHAPTER 2

Vaughn Darlington watched the coach vanish into the wintry night, his smile fading as the distance between him and Perdita Darby grew. He was a tad melancholy after the whirlwind of the last half hour. Part of him was still amused by the little beauty—her tenacity, her courage, even her recklessness in approaching someone with his reputation in his bedchamber. At midnight, no less.

A proposition, she'd said. And what a proposition it had been. The run of bad luck that had burdened him for so long seemed to be taking a turn for the better, and all because of a little country girl with sound intuition when it came to the darker side of Samuel Milburn.

His smile grew grim. She thought his announced interest in her would put off Milburn, but Vaughn knew Milburn better than she did. Whatever intentions Vaughn had for her, as his mistress or his betrothed, her scheme would not likely matter to a man like Milburn. He was a true bastard, a danger to the fairer sex, and would find a way to claim what he thought was rightfully his.

Yet Vaughn hadn't been able to tell her that whatever he did with her would not be enough to stop Milburn. Not on its own.

Vaughn could only hope their little charade would give him a chance to stop whatever Milburn was planning.

He considered the larger problem. Leverage. That was what Milburn had. So long as he held this evidence regarding Miss Darby's father, if it even existed, he would be in a position to pressure and cajole her. First, he would demand she break off her engagement, then bide his time before he held her feet to the fire to accept his own proposal. That sounded like the bastard's style. But without that evidence, his position would crumble.

He would put his butler on it. Craig was far more than he appeared to be, and he had not always been a butler. He had his ways of making men tell the truth. If anyone could get to the bottom of this, it was him.

His thoughts turned back to Perdita and her reaction to the nip he gave her shoulder. While Vaughn was quite notorious for his penchant for pain mixed with pleasure in bed play, he never harmed his bed partners. Milburn, however, had killed his last mistress, or so it was said. The rumors had been murmured in the seediest clubs, and once Vaughn heard he'd been disgusted with the man. Without proof, there wasn't enough to take the case to court. Milburn, as a gentleman, would escape prosecution.

The affair left a sour taste in Vaughn's mouth, which was why he'd agreed to help Perdita. He knew Milburn and his type. The man would stop at nothing until he was married to her, and then the law would do nothing once her new husband revealed his cruel streak.

Perdita was in danger, and the only way to remedy that was to offer her the ultimate protection—his name given in marriage. It was the reason he had taken so long to give her an answer. She had no idea that what she really needed was a true wedding, not a false engagement. And ordinarily, he would have declined.

But something about Perdita had changed his mind. It had happened ever so subtly over the course of their interaction. The way she'd softened in his arms when he'd kissed her. The way she'd challenged him when he'd reminded her of what her reputation would be like at the end of her charade. The way she was a charming and yet innocent country maiden who responded with fire and bravado. She'd intrigued him even as she'd stormed into his bedchamber, where there was no chaperone to save her from his clutches. None of it had been an act. Perdita was a woman worth knowing, a woman with secrets and passions and a mind all her own. *That* was a woman he could marry.

A smile crept back onto his face, and this time it was one of hesitant joy.

Vaughn walked into the drawing room and approached the tray of drinks his butler had set out earlier. He poured himself a glass of brandy before he took a seat in the chair by the fire just starting to turn to embers. He sipped his drink, savoring the flavor as he contemplated the unique opportunity Perdita had presented him with tonight.

It had been so long since he had looked forward to anything. Ever since his parents had died five years past, he'd been mired in debts that were too deep to recover from on his own. No matter what he did, he seemed to be damned. He'd had to close his country estate, let go of his entire staff save for one caretaker, and reduce the staff at his London townhouse.

His only way of getting by had been to win wagers at the clubs, and even that source was running dry. Every man in every major club now knew better than to wager large stakes when they found him across the gaming table. His ability to win should have helped pay off his family's debts, but not even the most gullible lads were foolish enough to stake their fortunes against him now.

He'd become known as the Devil of London in a matter of months. The moniker hadn't upset him as much as he thought it would at first, but it had kept men from playing even a simple game of cards with him. His friends certainly didn't approve of his actions, and in the last few years most had abandoned him.

Of course, he'd done other things, worse things, to drive his friends away. In the fall he had approached White's infamous betting book and found a five-thousand-pound sum wagered for publicly seducing a young woman named Alexandra Rockford, Perdita's close friend.

Kidnapping was not at all a charming prospect to him, unless of course the lady *wished* to be kidnapped. He'd played that particular game more than a few times with delightful results, but kidnapping Alexandra had been...*dreadful*.

He indulged in a moment of self-loathing. The night he had taken Alexandra to his home to fake her ruination for the sake of a wager had left a dark stain. He hated himself far more than he ever had before, and it showed how desperate he had truly become. That loathing had deepened until it left a scar on his heart. One he doubted would ever go away.

When he found Perdita in his doorway tonight, he hadn't expected to feel anything. Yet he had. She'd lowered her hood, and her brown hair had turned a burnished bronze in the lamplight. Her eyes, a gentle shade of brown like topaz stones, turned warm as honey. His blood had burned with desire in a way it hadn't in a long while. If that wasn't reason enough to marry the girl, he wasn't sure what else would be.

He left the drawing room and sought out his butler. He found the older man in his office on the basement of the townhouse.

"Mr. Craig, I have a task for you."

The butler glanced up from the papers on his desk. He gave Vaughn an appraising look. "Am I correct in assuming that this lies outside my usual duties?"

"You are."

Mr. Craig sighed. "I am no longer a young man, my lord."

"This is not for my own selfish desires, Mr. Craig. That young woman you brought to me requires our help. Her very life may depend on it."

Those words seemed to give Mr. Craig new vigor. He rose to his feet like a man twenty years younger. "Name it, my lord."

"A man named Samuel Milburn claims to have evidence that Mr. Reginald Darby has been involved in smuggling and evading taxes. He's using this as a means to pressure Darby's daughter into accepting marriage to him."

Mr. Craig scowled. Though he did not look it, he was at heart a romantic. In fact, Vaughn had caught him reading the works of L. R. Gloucester, a gothic novelist, on more than one occasion. The thought of any man forcing a woman by such means would be anathema to him.

"I want you to look into this. Miss Darby believes her father invested with men who might be working with Milburn. It could be they are trying to lay false evidence that Darby is the one behind the ill deeds. What we need is proof that Milburn is attempting to blackmail the Darby family, or proof of Mr. Darby's innocence. And if at all possible, I want you to put a stop to whoever is causing these problems, if you understand my meaning."

Mr. Craig's grim smile was a reminder of the man he'd once been, a man who'd fought valiantly for his country in the shadows years before.

"Understood."

He rarely spoke of those times, and when he did it was often in an allegorical fashion, but Vaughn had seen on more than one occasion just what Mr. Craig was capable of. And despite his complaints of old age and weariness, it took little to light the old fire under him again.

He left his butler and called for his valet, knowing the fellow would be up late.

"Barnaby!" His voice echoed in the darkened corridor. A few seconds later the man appeared around the edge of the door leading to the servants' quarters.

"My lord?"

"Pack me a valise for at least a week. We're going to Lothbrook in a few days and shall be there for Christmas." He tipped his brandy back and finished it before he headed for the stairs to return to his bedchamber.

Barnaby wrinkled his nose. "Lothbrook again? I'm still scraping the dust out of your trousers from the last visit, my lord." The man muttered this more to himself than to his master. Neither of them cared much for the country. It was so bloody provincial, but if he had to return there to seduce his unknowing bride, then that was where he must go.

He would deal with the details of his travel arrangements in the morning once he had had word from Perdita's parents that he was invited to their estate. With another small smile, he returned to his bedchamber and began to strip down for bed. He always slept in the buff, even in winter. It was a habit that would no doubt shock his little bride-to-be, but he suspected she would shock him right back. He closed his eyes, letting his mind flash images of her as he bent to kiss her, and the memory of it resurrected a smile upon his lips.

Her startled look, then the way she'd melted in his arms. She'd tasted like honey and fire, burning, yet impossibly sweet. He could still feel the velvet of her cloak, crumpled in his hands as he latched on to her. He had wanted to slide his hand up her skirts right then, but that would've been a step too far, no matter how she'd claimed she was not an innocent creature.

She was wanton, he would agree, yet still innocent in so many ways. Introducing Perdita to the mysteries of a man and woman coming together was not a thing to be rushed. Hasty fumblings in the dark would not do. No, she deserved a well-planned, deliciously slow seduction of the body and the mind.

Vaughn sat on the edge of his bed, raking his hands through his hair as he considered his next move. Tomorrow he needed to purchase a ring. He had little money to do so, but he'd find a way. His smile stretched into a broad grin. The invisible forces of fate had seemed determined to stop him from restoring his family's name in the *ton*, and now he had found a way to win against them: marry the *ton*'s darling. Miss Darby was the answer to his prayers. What a shock it would be to them all.

London's sweetest lady mated to its fiercest devil.

PERDITA STOOD BY HER MOTHER'S WRITING DESK IN HER PRIVATE sitting room, her heart racing more than it ought. Her mother sat at her delicate escritoire and was diligently checking the guest list for the party that would occupy their country estate in a few days. Perdita shifted about, her red shawl dropping from her shoulders to hang about her elbows and lower back.

"Perdita dear, you're lingering. You know how much I detest lingering. Either come and speak to me or be off."

Smoothing the skirts of her pale-rose gown, Perdita approached her mother and cleared her throat.

"I should like to add a guest to the list, Mama, if you don't mind. I know we have extra rooms." The estate was an ancient one that, while lacking the pomp of a peerage family with a title, was still a rival to many of the aristocratic homes in the country. It boasted no less than twenty bedrooms, a ballroom, and a music room. Perdita had numerous unpleasant memories of plucking away at a harp during an arranged musicale performance when she debuted two years ago.

Her mother glanced up, wisps of brown hair threaded with silver creeping out from her turban. "Oh? And who do you wish me to invite?"

Perdita straightened herself. "My fiancé."

The quill in her mother's hand seemed to hover a moment in midair before it clattered flat on the writing desk, splattering ink on the corner of the list her mother had been writing.

"Your..."

"Fiancé. Yes."

Her mother's eyes were as large as saucers. "So you accepted Mr. Milburn, then?"

"Er...no. It is someone else."

"What? But who?"

Perdita understood her mother's shock. It had been two long years since her debut, and she had rejected all offers that first year.

The second season she had not received any offers. Rather than become a spinster, she'd cultivated her reputation as a young lady of good character. Debutantes came to her for advice, society mamas sought the name of her modiste, and gentlemen sought her for conversations.

She was well versed to play the role set out for her. Charming and delightful, she was welcome in every London household. The one thing she had *not* done was allow herself to be courted. The men of England had given up, until Samuel Milburn met her a few months ago at a dinner party.

Their encounter had been brief, pointedly cool, at least from Perdita's side. Milburn had taken her cool aloofness in stride and informed her parents the following day of his intentions. Once Perdita learned of this, she'd come up with her desperate plan and had been biding her time until she felt safe enough to go to Vaughn.

"It's Lord Darlington, Mama. He and I have been seeing each other in secret. I know you disapprove of such things, but we wanted to be sure of our affections before we let society pry into our affairs."

Her mother's eyes nearly bulged out of her head. "Darlington? But... Good heavens, what about Milburn? I can't rescind his invitation for Christmas. He was most excited to come shooting with your father."

"I know..." Perdita pretended to consider the dilemma carefully, though she already knew her mind about it. "He must still come. However, we must also extend Lord Darlington an invitation."

Her mother picked up her quill and poised herself to write, but paused. "Are you quite sure, my dear? Lord Darlington is quite wicked, so I hear. I know I teased you in September about pursuing him, but it was only a jest."

"He is a viscount, Mama. His title will further us in society, will it not?"

"It will, but that's no reason to marry a man. If you loved him, that would be one thing, but if you don't, I wouldn't expect you to marry him."

Perdita held her breath, trying to summon the courage to lie to her mother, a thing she had never liked to do and avoided whenever possible.

"I love him, Mama, and I believe with a bit of time I can tame his restless spirit." She gave her mother an imploring look.

"Well, that is entirely possible, even of the worst rogues. I tamed your father, after all."

There was a loud *harrumph* from the doorway. Perdita turned to see her father standing there. He looked dapper in his blue breeches and waistcoat, his gray mustache twitching as he watched them.

"Tame *me?*" her father chortled. "Woman, you didn't tame me."

"I most certainly did!" Her mother stood, moving from her writing desk and to her husband. "You were a terrible rogue in your day, and it was quite the feat to bring you to your senses."

Perdita watched her parents with a blush in her cheeks.

"I only let you believe that." Her father's eyes twinkled as he caught Perdita's mother by her waist and pulled her close, kissing her cheek.

"Heavens, Reginald!" her mother hissed, but she was smiling as she chastised him. "Not here!"

"Very well." Reginald sighed dramatically. "Now, what's all this about taming men?"

"Well." Her mother waved at Perdita. "Your daughter seems to have gotten herself engaged and is only just now telling us."

"Milburn asked you, then?" Her father studied her curiously. His gaze was serious rather than delighted that his daughter had just announced she was to be married.

Perdita shook her head. "Um, no, actually. It was Lord Darlington. You remember him, don't you, Papa? He came to the garden party in September and stayed with us for a short time."

Papa raised one dark brow. "Darlington? You don't say..."

"Yes." Perdita's mother would be too blinded by the joy of

knowing her child was to be married, but her father was a little more levelheaded and might see through things.

"And you want to bring him for Christmas, is that it? Well, bring the lad so I can measure him and see if he is up to snuff. He ought to have come to me first, like that Milburn fellow did." Her father appeared to look stern, but there was a twinkle in his eyes that made Perdita want to laugh. If only she really were engaged. It was surprising to see how happy she had made her parents.

"We were keeping it a secret until we were sure of ourselves." Perdita pleaded with her eyes, hoping her father believed her. She needed Vaughn to come. She'd tried to mention Samuel Milburn's reputation to her father before, but he'd brushed it aside as idle talk. He knew all too well that gossip had been known to ruin lives unjustly and was disinclined to hear any more about it. It was one of the few times she'd ever been furious with him.

"Hmm, well, invite the boy, then." Her father kissed her mother's cheek and left them alone again.

"Perdita dear, I am most happy for you, of course, but are you quite sure Darlington is the one? I mean, you may have offers again from more than one gentleman. I was worried that..." Her mother trailed off, and heavy silence filled the room. It was only a matter of time before the *ton* tired of her and she was left on the shelf to become a spinster. She did not mind, but she knew her parents wished to see her happily married.

"Vaughn is the one for me." She used his given name purposefully, and it had the desired effect.

"Is it truly a love match? You know I only ever wanted a love match for you. That's why I always invite every young man I can find in hopes he might be perfect for you. Milburn seemed so attentive, and everyone spoke well of him. I had hopes that you might feel the same...but if your heart belongs to Lord Darlington, then that's settled, isn't it?"

Perdita clasped her mother's hands and squeezed them. She was a determined matchmaker for sport, but Perdita knew her mother's intentions were pure. She had married Papa for love and only wanted the same for her daughter. As often as her mother could be exasperating, she was also impossibly wonderful. That was why it hurt so much to lie to her.

"Yes. It is a love match. I never thought I'd win the heart of a man like Vaughn, but somehow I did."

"Win his heart?" Her mother chuckled. "You only need to win his mind first. It is he who must win *your* heart." Her mother squeezed her hands in return. "Very well, I shall invite your darling Darlington." She winked at Perdita and walked back to her desk to resume her guest list.

"If you don't mind, Mama, I am to have tea with Lady Lysandra Russell this afternoon at Gunter's."

"Of course." She returned her focus to her list. "Give her mother my regards, and take a footman with you."

"Thank you, Mama. Don't forget to send Darlington's invitation today. I wanted it to come from you so he would feel welcome."

"Consider it done." Her mother pulled a fresh bit of parchment toward her and began to scratch away with her quill, her turbaned head bowed.

Perdita called for Hensley, one of the young footmen, to bring her cloak and summon a coach. It would be too cold for ices, which Gunter's was most famous for. Tea would be preferable. They would also have to meet indoors. Gunter's was a treat when the weather was fine. A lady could arrive in Berkeley Square and remain in her open carriage while the men rushed from Gunter's to bring ices out to waiting customers. Indoors was perfectly fine for her intentions today. She and Lysandra had important things to discuss.

Hensley met her by the door and held out her dark-blue cloak. She slipped it on and took a white mink muff, tucking her hands inside. Then she and Hensley walked to the coach waiting for them.

When they reached Gunter's, Hensley came inside with her but kept his distance so she might enjoy her time alone with her friend. Lysandra Russell was waiting, a tea service in front of her at one of the tables. Her bright-red hair was like a flame that danced in the lamplight of the shop. Lysandra didn't seem to notice the appreciative stares of the men around them. But that was just how Lysa was, her head buried in books, her mind preoccupied with their shared purpose.

"Lysa." Perdita took an empty chair opposite her friend at the small tea table.

"Oh! Perdita, forgive me." Lysa blushed and raised her head from her stack of letters. She tucked the letters into her lap and poured a cup of tea for her friend.

"Thank you." Perdita slipped the muff off her hands and sipped her tea.

Lysa beamed. "Our paper on the astronomical developments of the last few months is ready for publication. I believe we might be accepted this time." Lysa grinned and nodded at the pen name they had chosen to hide their genders: P. L. Bottomsley.

"I've drafted a proper introduction. Officially, we are a gentleman from Tintagel, Cornwall. I've acquired the use of an address there. There's a man named Mikhail Barinov. He's agreed to collect any correspondence and deliver it to London first. I believe this time we shall have our ducks in a row. The Astronomy Society of London *must* publish us."

Perdita couldn't help but smile as well. This was her dream—their observations and scientific discoveries published. As ladies and not learned gentleman scholars, their articles had been continually rejected. And so, a ruse had to be devised. The need for it was maddening.

"Brilliant, Lysa." Perdita took the article and reviewed the neatly written words, checking each page carefully. Then she handed it back to Lysa, who tucked it into a leather folio.

"I will submit it on the morrow with the messenger and let you know once I hear if we've been successful."

"Excellent." Perdita glanced around the shop, her eyes taking in the couples having tea. Gunter's was one of the few places in

London a lady could meet with a gentleman alone and not worry about scandal or ruination. The door opened with a small bell tinkling as a group of men came in from the cold. Perdita recognized one of them, and her heart pitched straight to her feet.

Samuel Milburn was here.

"Lysa, I'm so sorry, but I must leave immediately." She nodded discreetly at Samuel, who was removing his hat and coat.

Lysa's eyes settled on the man as she nodded. "Of course. Good luck."

Perdita waved Hensley over.

"Miss?" Hensley asked, brushing crumbs from his trousers.

"I'd like to leave. Please have the coach brought around at once."

Hensley pulled his coat on and ducked outside. Perdita carefully walked around the edge of the tea shop, weaving between the couples and tables, trying to keep out of Samuel's sight. She pulled her hood up and reached the door just in time to overhear part of his conversation with the other gentlemen.

"You've still not proposed to the Darby chit yet?" one of the men asked.

Samuel chuckled. "Not officially. I'm waiting for Christmas. Women love that sort of romantic drivel. I also need to make sure she's mine. I have to be able to have her before I make my decision. There's enough fire in her that I believe she'd be a pleasure to break. Have to make sure though. She might be one of those weepy virginal debutantes. Can't have that. I want her to fight me before I break her completely."

His companions laughed, one comparing such "sport" with the hunting of a wild animal.

Milburn sneered. "Indeed, except one must be stuffed before it is mounted, while the other must be mounted in order to be stuffed."

The grating sound of their harsh laughter made Perdita nearly toss up her accounts. She couldn't bear to hear another word. She rushed out into the cold, not caring if the biting wind tore at her face. Samuel's threats were unimaginable. How could the *ton* be so blinded by him not to see his evil? Yet she feared that was the sort of darkness lying in his soul. He was a man with no heart, and he cared for nothing except his own needs. She would not become his victim; she would do anything to escape such evil. Vaughn would be her salvation. She trusted him, something which should have been surprising, yet it did not feel so.

Evil and sorrow left very different shadows on a man's face. Evil was a malignant presence that smothered and strangled the goodness around it. But it was different with sorrow. Vaughn's eyes were painted in shadows of pain and loss. It was a shadow that might someday be vanquished by the rays of the sun. She had glimpsed the hope of it in his eyes when she'd kissed him last night, like sunlight streaking through the parted curtains of a mansion that had been shrouded in darkness for eons. It was foolish, she knew, to take pleasure in knowing their kiss might've lessened his sorrows, whatever they were, but she did.

Perdita looked around for Hensley and saw with some relief the coach was already approaching. She could not wait another minute this close to Samuel. He and his companions had confirmed her worst nightmares.

Thank heavens for Vaughn.

Hensley had their driver stop the coach, and he helped her inside. The velvet cushions were cold, but she sighed in relief when Hensley placed a foot warmer at her feet.

"Where to now, miss?" Hensley asked.

"Home, I suppose." She parted the curtains on the opposite side of the square, but then she held up a hand. "Wait. Stay here. I should like to go to that shop. The one just there."

She pointed at the little jewelry shop across the street. She could have sworn she'd seen Vaughn entering it. Had she been dreaming merely because she was thinking of him just now? There was only one way to find out.

CHAPTER 3

S he climbed back out of the coach, heading directly for the row of shops. If it was Vaughn, she needed to tell him what she'd overheard in Gunter's. He had a right to know Samuel's intentions. He might have an idea of how to protect her against the man since Samuel had made it clear he wanted to get her alone.

Hensley closed the coach door behind her and followed her as she passed a milliner's shop and reached the jeweler's. She peered into the windows, which were frosted around the edges from the cold, but she couldn't see Vaughn.

Perhaps he'd gone deeper into the shop. She tugged on the brass door handle. It creaked open, and she slipped inside. The little shop was warm, but a faint musty smell emanated from the shelves where a variety of necklaces hung on stands and both bracelets and rings were displayed in glass cases. It was clear from the designs that these jewelry items were old, not newly fashioned.

Perdita peered around the shop, searching for Vaughn. She paused behind a row of tall shelves, considering the possibility that she'd only seen a gentleman who bore a passing resemblance to him.

A voice came from the other side of the wall of jewels behind which Perdita stood. "My lord, what may I do for you?"

Perdita perked up at the sound and was prepared to seek out the jeweler, but something held her back. She stayed hidden and peered between the dusty shelves, fighting the need to sneeze with one hand. She glimpsed an elderly shopkeeper with a hooked nose and spectacles speaking with a tall man with dark-blond hair. The man stood with his back to her, but Perdita was positive it was Vaughn.

"What can I get for this?" Vaughn held out a pocket watch, a very old but beautiful piece. Its silver cover glinted with light as it swung from a fine chain. The jeweler took it and held it up, leaving Vaughn to shift slightly. His face turned away from the jeweler, offering Perdita a glimpse of his profile and the pain etched in his features.

"Well now, let me take a look." The jeweler paused to push his glasses up the bridge of his nose and studied the watch closely.

"Finely made, with the Darlington family crest... Forty pounds, I should think. Are you quite sure you want to part with it, my lord?" The jeweler eyed the watch and then Vaughn. Perdita held her breath. Hensley shifted behind her, and she threw out a hand, catching his arm and raising her other hand to her lips to indicate silence. She did not want to interrupt whatever Vaughn was doing.

It appeared as though he was selling off his family heirlooms. Given the condition of his home—the lack of furnishings and general disrepair—it shouldn't have surprised her. However, if she was being honest, she didn't want to think of Vaughn as so destitute he was selling such a personal item. Her heart gave a painful twinge as she held her breath, listening.

"Forty? I suppose that's a fair enough price. Is there a ring which I might trade it for?" Vaughn set the pocket watch on the counter between him and the jeweler. His fingers didn't immediately let go of the watch. Perdita's heart gave another painful jerk. He was looking at rings? Why would he wish to sell a watch for a ring?

Then a thought struck her. Was the ring for her?

The jeweler lifted a velvet box onto the counter. "These here are quite lovely." Perdita stood on tiptoe to get a better view. She was thankful the shelves were open for her to peer through.

"This one here, is it a ruby?" Vaughn pointed at a ring. She couldn't see which because his body was blocking her view.

"Yes, a fine ruby. I suppose we could make a fair trade for the watch," the jeweler said.

"Good." Vaughn nudged the watch toward him. "Do you have a box for it?"

"I do." The jeweler disappeared into the back and moments later emerged with a small blue velvet box. He placed the ring inside and handed it back to Vaughn.

"Thank you." Vaughn took the box and tucked it securely into his coat and lifted his hat off the counter.

"Good day, my lord," the jeweler said as Vaughn turned toward the door—and Perdita. Perdita grasped Hensley and propelled him around the opposite end of the shelf, just missing being seen by Vaughn as he left. Once she was sure Vaughn was no longer inside, she and Hensley moved around the shelf and approached the counter where Vaughn had stood. The jeweler was still putting the set of rings back beneath the glass display counter.

"Oh! Good day, miss" the jeweler said. "I didn't realize you'd come in. How may I assist you?" He brushed his hands on his apron and readjusted his glasses with a warm smile.

Perdita noticed Vaughn's watch still sitting on the counter and tried to act slightly interested. "This is a lovely watch. May I see it?" she asked.

The jeweler eyed her quizzically. "The old pocket watch?"

She nodded, chancing one glance at the door. There was no sign of Vaughn returning.

"Of course." The jeweler set the watch down on the counter so Perdita could examine it. It was indeed an old watch, possibly Vaughn's father's or even his grandfather's. How could he bear to part with it? For a ring, no less?

She hadn't thought what it meant to provide evidence to support their story of an engagement. Had Vaughn believed he needed proof such as this? Or was it for a mistress? For some reason, she didn't think so. If he was as destitute as she now believed, he could not afford a mistress. That left her with the sad knowledge that the ring must be for her, and he had sold his watch for it. She had to buy it back. He had sold the watch, one she suspected was dear to him, for a ring she believed he meant to give to her. Therefore, she would make sure he got his watch back when the time was right. Vaughn was a proud man, and she would not endanger his pride by letting him know she'd witnessed this moment.

"How much for it?"

"Pardon, miss?" The jeweler's brows rose.

"How much to buy the watch? I'd like to buy it." She didn't want Vaughn to lose one of the last pieces of his family's past if she could help it.

"Well...I believe fifty pounds is fair."

She met his gaze. "But you traded it for forty."

"Forty-five then," the jeweler countered.

She lifted her chin. "Forty-two."

The jeweler stuck out his chin as well. "Forty-three."

"Agreed." She lifted her reticule onto the counter and counted out the notes. She rarely carried large sums of money, but she had planned to do a bit of shopping today after meeting with Lysandra. She hadn't expected it to be for her false fiancé.

She had the jeweler wrap it for her and then entrusted the box to Hensley.

"We're going home now, miss?" His hesitant tone implied his hope at the thought.

"Not a lover of clandestine meetings or secret missions, Hensley?" she teased. The footman, a man close to her age, blushed to the roots of his hair.

"It isn't that, miss... I just worry about you, is all."

The footman's honest comment caught her off guard.

"Worry about me?" she asked. He was unable to meet her eyes.

"I shouldn't have said that, miss. My apologies." He continued to avoid her gaze, and she didn't force him to speak of it further. Mostly because she was afraid to hear what he would say. There was an infuriating pity that came from servants when they dealt with spinsters, as though even downstairs they felt sorry for the unmarried maids who aged on the shelf.

The thought made her sour. Women had a right to aspire to other positions than simply being a wife and mother, did they not? Yet those were the only positions society valued for them. It wasn't her fault she didn't wish to be seen as a broodmare. The idea filled her with a defiant purpose. Once she and Vaughn were done with this charade and Milburn had lost interest, she would devote herself to seeing her astronomy essays published.

"We have one more stop to make," Perdita announced. "Have the driver take us to Half Moon Street." Then she climbed into the coach and listened for Hensley to give orders to the driver.

She peered eagerly out of the coach window as they reached Lennox House. It was a stunningly built structure that emanated both power and beauty. Her warm breath clouded the glass. She rubbed her gloved hand on the window to remove some of the fog for a better look.

The coach came to a stop, and Perdita instructed Hensley to wait with the driver for her. Depending on how furious her friend Rosalind was at her request, it was possible Perdita would be cast back into the street. A small bout of nerves rose up in her, but she shoved them down. The two were friends, and although she had not had a chance to visit Rosalind since she'd married Lord Lennox and moved into his house, things shouldn't have changed much, or so she hoped.

She rapped the large silver knocker and waited. The butler answered, and she was relieved to be allowed in once he had made the proper inquiries.

The butler directed her to a drawing room. Rosalind was working at a writing desk by the fire.

"Perdita." Rosalind rose once she entered the room. "How are you?" Her voice lilted with a Scottish accent, one she no longer tried to hide as much as she used to. The accent rendered the dark-haired woman utterly charming with a touch of that Highland wildness.

"I am well, and you?"

"Very well." Rosalind's gray eyes twinkled. "Have you come to discuss your investments?"

"Yes, well, possibly. It is a matter of business, but it is also a bit delicate in nature."

Her friend's open smile turned to a frown. "Shall we sit?" Rosalind led her to a dark-red brocade settee and poured a cup of tea from a pot on the table.

"Thank you." Perdita steeled herself for what she had to do. It was not like her to make such requests of friends.

Rosalind seemed to notice her hesitation. "We are friends, Perdita. Ask whatever you came to ask."

"It is a rather long tale, but I shall try to be brief. I'm trying to escape an engagement to Samuel Milburn, whose intentions I do not trust. I do not wish to go into details, but I am under some rather unsavory pressure to accept. I made a bargain with Viscount Darlington to act as my fiancé in order to put Milburn off. But Darlington's price in aiding me is..." She choked on the words, hating to have to speak this way to a friend. "Well, his fortunes have taken a poor turn, and he wishes me to ask for your husband to involve him in his next investment." There. She'd said it, even though it left a bitter taste upon her tongue.

For a long moment, Rosalind didn't speak, her brows furrowed as she studied Perdita carefully. Did she think Perdita was only trying to use her? Was she reconsidering their friendship?

"Darlington, you say?" Rosalind pursed her lips and thought. "I haven't met him, but I've heard of him. Bit of a wild fellow. Are you sure you want to attach yourself to him so publicly?"

Perdita sipped her tea and nodded. "Despite what you may have heard of Samuel Milburn, I assure you that man is a brute. He has every intention of breaking me if he can compromise me into marriage."

"*Break* you?"

"My spirit, and perhaps more."

Rosalind's pensive gaze turned into a scowl. "I haven't heard much about this Milburn fellow, but if he has you frightened, we shan't let him succeed in putting you in a position where you must marry him." She lifted a small bell from her tea tray and rang it. A footman appeared, and Rosalind spoke. "Please tell my husband I wish to speak with him."

The servant bowed and vanished.

"Is there really no way other than to enlist Lord Darlington's help? I'm sure you've heard the rumors about him," Rosalind said.

"I have, but I believe there may be more to him than the rumors give him credit for. When presented with a situation such as I have given him, he wished to help and asked only this favor in return. It's not what I expected of a notorious rogue, but I trust him. Does that sound very strange and foolish?"

"To trust a rogue? That is neither strange nor foolish, if it's the right rogue. I will ask my husband what he knows of Darlington."

"Thank you, Rosalind. I cannot tell you how much I appreciate your help. It's so upsetting to have to ask it of you."

"Nonsense. This is precisely what friends are for." Rosalind covered Perdita's hand and gave it a gentle pat.

Lord Lennox appeared a moment later. He was a tall man with piercing blue eyes and blond hair, not unlike Vaughn, but there was a wild desperation to Vaughn that Lennox did not share. He was calm, relaxed, *settled*. Vaughn had a leaner appearance to him and a grimness to his bearing that gave him a melancholy darkness.

"You summoned me?" While Ashton's tone was cool, his lips were curled in a teasing smile. He came over to Rosalind and pressed a kiss to her hand.

"This is my dear friend, Perdita Darby. She is also a customer of our bank," Rosalind explained. "Perdy, please tell my husband what you told me."

Perdita detailed what she had guessed of Samuel Milburn and his intentions, as well as her scheme with Darlington and the favor required as payment for his services.

"I've met him a few times around London. Not a bad fellow, or so I hear," Lennox mused. "Milburn, on the other hand...well, I've heard about his mistress. The one who fell to her death. An accident, they say, but I'm not sure I believe that."

Perdita nodded.

"So, Darlington is keen to invest with me?" Ashton leaned back in his chair thoughtfully. "He wouldn't be the first, but there are good reasons why I am selective about whom I take into my confidence. Most believe the risks I take are too great, but they simply do not understand my longer plans and fail to see that in the end there is very little risk at all. But I require trust, and not all are willing to give it. I will not have my every action second-guessed. I believe he'd make a good partner. He has a good head on his shoulders, and I understand he was quite successful before his parents passed. The debts they left him with were extraordinary and ruined his own small fortune."

Lennox shared a long glance with Rosalind before he stood and nodded.

"Very well, tell Darlington he may call upon me after the New Year. I shall discuss my next venture with him, and he can decide then if he still wishes to take part."

His words were such a relief that Perdita was overcome with gratitude. "Thank you, Lord Lennox. Truly."

"Any friend of Rosalind's is a friend of mine." He kissed her hand, and with a lingering glance at his wife, which made the lady blush, he left them alone.

"Silly man," Rosalind muttered, though she was smiling.

Perdita had to agree. Lord Lennox was a silly, wonderful man. *Wait until I tell Vaughn. He'll be so pleased.* She had guaranteed not just an introduction, but involvement in Lennox's next venture. Perhaps she would survive Christmas after all.

CHAPTER 4

Vaughn felt naked without his pocket watch. It had been a few days since he'd sold it, and he and Barnaby were now headed to Lothbrook. He kept reaching into his coat for the watch, and his hand came back empty.

The piece had belonged to his grandfather, handcrafted by Thomas Mudge himself, and it had been given to him by his own father when he turned sixteen. He'd had it for so long he'd forgotten what it was like not to have it sitting securely in his waistcoat pocket. It was the last thing of any real value he had left to sell.

But obtaining a ring for his future bride had been important. It sat safely in his coat pocket, but he kept checking the box to make sure it hadn't vanished. Between his secret plan to actually seduce her for her fortune and using her to become acquainted with Baron Lennox, he was already indebted to her.

Vaughn was not a man who liked to owe a debt. The ring was his last chance to prove he could offer her something before he ended up owning everything that had once been hers. Even if he had something else left to sell, he couldn't stomach visiting that jeweler's shop again. *Selling my past to secure my future.* He only hoped it would work.

The coach he sat in was stuffed with people like hens in a coop, but a damned public coach was all he could afford. Farmers sat on either side of him, their shoulders pressing into his. The odor of the barnyard was rather too pungent for Vaughn to stomach. He'd taken turns holding his breath and attempting to breathe through his mouth. It helped, but *only* just.

The coach came to a halt at the crossroads, and the driver shouted that they'd reached Lothbrook. Despite the press of bodies, he was chilled to the bone from the icy wind that cut through the coach's cracks. Vaughn surged out of the coach, his boots crunching into a light layer of snow. He stretched his legs, relieved to be away from the crush of the vehicle and its occupants.

The town was covered in snow, the roofs of the shops and houses capped with ice. The skies were dark with wintry clouds that seemed to stretch the darkness across the village and swallow up the meager lights from lamps still sitting in windowsills.

Lord, he missed Lothbrook in the late summer. Even when he'd been here last September, the town had been full of flowers, and the days had seemed endless.

"Oi!" The driver's shout caught Vaughn's attention. He spun in time to see Barnaby rush to catch the valises the driver had unceremoniously dropped to the ground. Vaughn scowled as he and Barnaby collected their cases and walked toward the edge of town.

"What a tosser!" Barnaby muttered as he tramped alongside Vaughn, carrying one of the cases while Vaughn managed the other.

"Agreed," Vaughn said. "But it is the season of forgiveness. And if all goes well, dear Barnaby, we shall never have to suffer travel by public coach again."

"Humph. That's *assuming* you win Miss Darby's heart, my lord. She's a crafty chit, that one," Barnaby noted. Other men might have cuffed a servant for such frankness, but Vaughn had always preferred to employ those with a mind to speak up and share observations. They also tended to be cheaper.

"I think I stand a fair chance. She was quite taken with me the other night." Vaughn puffed out his chest and ignored his valet rolling his eyes. He hadn't imagined Perdita's impassioned reaction to his kiss or his touch. He was an excellent lover and had never mistaken a woman's passion.

The Darby estate was not far, but in the cold...well, it wasn't exactly a pleasant stroll. By the time they set foot on the long stone path that led to the Darbys' country house, Vaughn's feet were frozen, and he couldn't feel his face. The merry candlelight framed in the windows beckoned him forward, and he knocked upon the door. A footman opened the door, bracing himself against the cold.

"Pardon me, my lord, but you are Lord Darlington, correct? Miss Darby has been expecting you and feared you might run late," the young man replied. Damnation, he'd wished to arrive earlier than this. *Bloody public coaches. If we hadn't had to stop every three miles to let off farmers and their damned chickens, we wouldn't have been late.*

"Yes." Vaughn hastened up the steps and gratefully had Barnaby hand them his luggage. Another footman took his hat and coat.

The numerous servants who dashed about the house were all decked out in fine winter livery. They passed several maids on their way up the stairs, and Vaughn swallowed a pang of guilt for his one beleaguered little maid, Pippa, who was responsible for a town-house that should retain at least a dozen more. That would be one of the first things he changed if he could get a successful return on his future investments with Lennox.

"Please, this way. I'll show you to your room. I'm afraid you've missed dinner, but Miss Perdita insisted you have a full tray brought to your room when you arrived."

"Did she now?" He was surprised at her thoughtfulness, but then again, between her and her friend Alexandra, Perdita was the sweeter of the two. Alexandra...now *that* woman had a cornered badger's temper.

Vaughn followed the footman up the stairs, Barnaby trailing behind, muttering about old, cold country houses. They were shown to an elegant chamber, the same one he'd stayed in before when he'd come down for the garden party in September. The large bed looked warm and inviting, as did the fire in the hearth. Thick Aubusson carpets covered the floors, making the room feel cozy.

His own chambers back in London were in a severe state of disrepair, not at all like the dark oak wainscoting here, which contrasted with the dark-green embossed wallpapers with gold ivy patterns. Even the bed hangings, a rich brocade of dark gold, matched the coverlet and sheets.

After the footman left, Barnaby set about putting away his master's clothes in a large wardrobe. By the way his valet sighed wistfully, he knew the young man missed having real furnishings as much as he did.

Barnaby approached the shaving stand, where hot water stood ready in a pristine blue-and-white basin. Clean clothes and face towels were neatly folded next to a bar of expensive milled soap. The valet turned back to him, a little streak of guilt flashing in his brown eyes.

"Perhaps the country isn't as bad as you remember?" Vaughn said with a rueful smile.

"No, my lord." Barnaby's face turned red, and he hastily resumed his work.

Vaughn leaned back against the bed and sighed. Part of him still couldn't believe he was here. But he truly was desperate enough to accept Perdita's offer of a false engagement, because he knew he could seduce her into wanting a real one. Women were quite easy to woo, after all, so long as they weren't in love with another, as Alexandra had been. Of course, should Perdita deny her own desires for him, he would at least still have the meeting with Lennox to help secure his future.

Vaughn straightened as a worried thought streaked through his mind. Was it possible that Perdita already loved another?

Surely if she did, she would have convinced *that* man to participate in this game, not him. With a low growl, Vaughn retrieved the ring and tucked the box into a drawer in one of the night tables by the bed.

He turned at a soft knock upon the bedroom door.

"Enter."

The door opened, and Perdita slipped inside, followed by a footman with a tray.

"Lord Darlington, I wanted to make sure you've been properly seen to. Set the tray on the table, please, Hensley." She gestured to the mahogany fireside table. The footman set the tray down before departing.

Vaughn was momentarily distracted by the sight of the covered dishes. His nose picked up the scents of soup, fresh bread, roast beef, potatoes, and peas. He even glimpsed a berry tart on a small plate. God bless the woman—real food was just what he needed after his long journey.

He forced his thoughts away from the food for a moment, no matter how much his stomach grumbled about it. He approached a fine Chinese lacquer commode in the corner of the room, which contained decanters of brandy and whisky.

"Care for a drink?" he offered, hoping she would sit with him in the two leather chairs facing the fire.

"No, thank you," she replied. Perdita played with her skirts, and the nervous movement almost made him smile. Her dress was blue, with Van Dyke sleeves trimmed with Belgian lace. Her bodice and hem were dusted with silver embroidery, and a lock of her dark hair dangled loose upon the creamy skin of her neck. The woman looked positively edible, like Christmas pudding and a glass of sherry.

"Perdita." He spoke her name, unsure what else to say before he asked the question that was now plaguing him.

She inclined her head. "Vaughn." There was a long silence between them before he approached her.

"There is no other man, is there?" he asked, his heart pounding as he waited for her to reassure him this entire charade wasn't a fool's errand.

Her brows knit in confusion. "Other man?"

"Yes. One you love, who for some reason isn't riding in here on a bloody white charger to save you from Samuel Milburn."

She paled and her fists clenched. A blush replaced the pallor in her cheeks. "No, of course there isn't another. If there was, I would be engaged, not begging someone like you to help me."

He tilted his head. "Someone like *me*? What, pray tell, makes me the fortunate man for this situation?"

Perdita glared at him. "Because... Wait, why are you asking me this *now*? I thought we'd agreed to this..." The look of anger faded to panic, and for some reason that cut into the thick wall around his frozen heart, warming it ever so slightly.

"I did agree," he said. "I merely wish to make sure that I'm not doing this when someone else should be. If there's another who loves you, he should be here. Not me."

Perdita blew out a breath. "No. There's no one. It's why I need you."

Bloody hell, that shouldn't have aroused him, yet it did. The thought of her needing him, even in this way, was enough to fill his head with wicked thoughts that would send her running if she could only read his mind at that moment. He wanted to make her need him in a thousand other ways, until her body could no longer bear the touch of another because only his would satisfy her. He pushed the rush of hungry thoughts aside and focused on their conversation.

"And here I am, minus the white horse, in my rusted armor." He gave her a mocking bow.

She curtseyed elegantly in return. "I suppose that makes me a damsel in a dire state of distress? Good heavens, I'm the heroine of a gothic novel."

"So it would seem." He caught her hand, lifting it to his lips. "I should love to see you fleeing down some darkened corridor, your hair unbound, your body clad only in the flimsiest of nightgowns, clutching a candelabra as you flee from a dark stranger. I would take you into my arms and rescue you. Then, of course, I would make mad passionate love to you so that all worries of dark strangers would be forgotten."

Her pupils widened as he spoke. He took a moment to caress the back of her hand with his fingertips as he watched, drinking in every minute expression of hers.

She seemed torn between laughter and consternation. "*That's* what I am rewarded with? You coming here just to seduce me? I waited a fortnight for you, made sure the cook prepared the best supper fresh for you, and—"

Vaughn didn't let her finish. It had always been his policy to silence a chattering woman the most pleasurable way he knew how. He pulled one arm around her waist and tugged her into his arms. She gasped against his lips, and he couldn't resist smiling.

Lord, she tasted divine. She shivered against him, and he slid one hand through her hair, tugging lightly on the strands. Perdita whimpered and curled an arm around his neck, kissing him back harder.

Seducing her was going to be easy.

He slid his other hand down her body, cupping her backside, then gave it a playful smack. She jolted, and he winced when her teeth sank into his lip.

"Ow!" He pulled back, letting her go as he touched where his lip stung. Perdita steadied herself against the nearest chair, brushing her loosened hair back from her face. He had ruined her coiffure, and she looked as though she'd been thoroughly tumbled in bed. It was a good look for her—soft, vulnerable, and a bit mussed. He licked his sore lip and grinned.

"You don't want a bit of compromise with your engagement? I am ready to offer *all* of my services, not just my reputation." He waggled his eyebrows at her.

"You *struck* me!"

He flashed a crooked smile. "I spanked you, darling. There's quite a difference. Tell me you didn't feel the jolt when I did." He knew she'd deny it, and he was going to enjoy proving her wrong over the next several days.

"I felt nothing!" she snapped.

"Then why are you complaining if you felt nothing?" he teased, twisting her words.

She spun on her heel and headed for the door. "Oh!"

He caught her from behind and pulled her back as he closed the door, trapping her in his arms. "Perdy, wait."

"Do not call me Perdy," she growled and turned to look over her shoulder at him. Their noses brushed, and her eyes flashed with a beautiful fire. It made him hot all over.

"Why not? I know Alexandra calls you that." He smiled as his gaze lowered to her lips. She turned to face him, smacking his chest with her hand.

"Because she is my friend. Friends call me Perdy, but not you." He had to bite back a groan of hunger seeing the fire in her eyes just then. When had a woman's eyes ever been so captivating? He couldn't recall a time before this when he was so fascinated by a woman's gaze.

"We aren't friends," he agreed. "But we are affianced, aren't we?" He caught one of her wrists and brought her hand to his lips, kissing her palm.

"What are you doing?" But she was staring at him as he kissed her palm. Then he began to work kisses up her arm, inch by inch.

"Reminding you"—he paused to kiss her between each set of words—"that we...need to get...more comfortable...with each other...and that means...more of...*this*." He tilted her head up and pressed a slow kiss to her stunned lips.

He could hear the little growl she made and felt it as it rumbled from her chest. There was nothing more delightful than proving a woman wrong about her desires. It wasn't about force, but about slow, thoughtful seduction. Not only of the body, but of the mind and heart as well.

He kissed her for another long moment, waiting until he felt her melting into him, and then he released her. She stood there, eyes glazed with desire, lips swollen, hair delightfully mussed, and her skirts wrinkled where he'd clenched the fabric tight to keep his own frayed control in check.

"I have something for you." He walked to the night table and retrieved the ring. Perdita was pale again, her eyes fixed on the little velvet box.

"Vaughn, you didn't need to—"

"I did and I wanted to. Even if this engagement is false, I would still provide my bride with a token of my affection." He held the box out. He did not kneel, nor did he present it with any fanfare. That simply wasn't the sort of man he was. If she couldn't see what he was offering her and understand the sacrifice he had made, then she wasn't the woman he had thought she was.

She took the box from him, their hands meeting briefly, yet still causing a spark at their touch. He watched her face as she opened the box, memorizing every detail. The way her eyes darkened the moment she spied the ruby ring, the way she tilted her head, the loose curl bouncing against her neck and shoulders, and finally the way her lips parted on a soft gasp.

"Vaughn, no, this is too precious. You must not give me this. Not simply to further a charade." She took a tiny step toward him, the open box held out. He reached up and clasped her hands, closing them over it.

He captured her eyes with his, letting her see how serious he was. "I insist."

"But—"

"No," he responded in a clipped tone. He knew what she intended to say—that he had so little to give as it was—but he *needed* her to have this, even if he could not bring himself to explain why. There were some things a man could not share with his intended bride.

Perdita opened the box again and looked at the ring. "It's very lovely." When she spoke there was a small catch in her voice, and it made his chest clench and his throat tighten.

This is all I can give you. The last of what I have left.

"You like it?" He felt like a fool, begging for scraps of her attention, needing to hear that the sacrifice of his grandfather's pocket watch had not been in vain. She traced the ruby stone and the two small diamonds flanking it, bit her lip, and nodded.

"I do. I don't believe I've ever owned anything so lovely." She paused, and then with a radiant smile at him, she asked, "May I wear it now, or must I wait until Christmas?"

He cleared his throat, that strange tightness still there, making it hard to speak.

"Now is fine, quite fine," he finally managed.

She plucked the ring from the box and slid it on her ring finger.

It was almost a perfect fit, with just a bit of looseness, which could be easily remedied when she visited the jeweler in the village. The ruby gleamed in the firelight.

"Thank you." Perdita stood up on her tiptoes and kissed him. The lingering sweet taste of her felt different from any other kiss. This wasn't one of lust, desire, or anger. This was simply *something else*. It evoked a flutter of strange and unidentifiable emotions in him that he didn't want to think about.

A rose hue accented her cheekbones as she touched her lips. "Eat your dinner before it gets cold, and rest well. Tomorrow the holiday festivities begin in earnest, and I shall need my white knight at my side, rusty armor or no."

Without another word, she was gone, leaving Vaughn to stare after her, his hands twitching with the sense they missed holding her.

CHAPTER 5

Perdita lingered in the hallway, watching the coaches pull up outside. Ladies in cloaks and men in greatcoats ascended the steps to the house. Her parents stood ready to greet their guests. Perdita stayed back, slightly distracted, wondering when Vaughn was going to come down. He had ordered a tray for breakfast early that morning, so she'd missed seeing him at the table. After last night, she felt oddly nervous and a bit excited.

Because he's dangerous and the charade you're playing is far too exhilarating. Her inner voice was happy to chastise her for her foolish behavior around Vaughn. But she hadn't forgotten why she was doing this. To save Papa, as well as herself.

She twisted the ruby ring on her finger, even though it felt quite comfortable there. Vaughn had given it to her, not someone else. To think she'd been worried about him buying it for another woman. A hint of a smile escaped her lips, but she wiped it away. This thing between her and Vaughn was nothing more than a cunning deception, and she had to remember that. She would return the ring and his pocket watch once this was all was over. It was the least she could do.

Her mother called to her. "Perdy, dear, come and see to the

guests." She joined her parents with a sigh and a forced air of happiness. A pair of men rode up on horseback, their fine beasts kicking at the fresh snow that had fallen early that morning. She started to smile as they approached, but she halted. Her slippers slid on the snowy steps as she recognized one of the men.

Samuel Milburn had arrived. Fear spiked inside her, and she fought the urge to turn and run.

"Miss Darby." Samuel came up the steps, grinning.

To everyone but her, he appeared to be nothing more than a handsome man with dark hair and dark-brown eyes, with no hint of the real darkness within him. But she knew it was there. She'd heard him herself in Gunter's, laughing with his companions about how he would enjoy breaking her. There was a darkness in his eyes, one that promised pain, not just for her but for her family if she defied him. It was the look of a man who believed he held all the cards and was simply biding his time before collecting his winnings. Knowing what she did about him made Perdita want to run and hide, even though she usually preferred to stand and fight.

She would be damned if she'd let him turn her into property by blackmailing her. However, he was a guest, and she could not prove his evil inclinations to her parents, so she would simply have to be careful during the house party.

That was why Vaughn was here. She hoped his very presence would protect her in ways she could not manage on her own. As much as she hated relying on a man, she felt she could trust him in this matter. And he seemed to know the sort of man Samuel was and thought the man a bastard, just as she did.

"Mr. Milburn, welcome," Perdita said, her tone cool but polite. There was no need to anger him, not if the charade with Vaughn was to succeed. The goal was to simply remove his interest in her, not provide him with reasons to desire retribution.

"Thank you, Miss Darby. I trust you have given thought to what we spoke of when last we met?" He flashed a charming grin that didn't fool her one bit. She did not miss the look of calculation he gave her or the way he eyed her critically from head to toe, the way a man would study a horse he planned to acquire at Tattersall's.

"I have." It was all she would admit to. The time to reveal her engagement had not yet come, and she wouldn't let it slip until Vaughn decided the time was right. He knew how to deal with a man like Milburn.

She stepped back and let him pass, along with his companion. Another coach was arriving, and she was relieved to have an excuse to leave Mr. Milburn to be seen to his room.

Another dozen guests arrived before Perdita was allowed to retire to her room before lunch was served. She decided to stay in her light-green wool gown with red trimming on the sleeves and hem. Most of the ladies would be changing out of their carriage dresses, but since she hadn't traveled, she would do well enough in her day gown.

The entire notion of changing one's dress three or four times a day frustrated her. There were a dozen other things she would prefer to accomplish on any given day, and having to change to suit the time of day or activity was both bothersome and unnecessary. Men didn't have to change clothes so frequently, and she was envious of that freedom.

She chose to visit the library on the second floor on the opposite wing of the house, hoping to catch a glimpse of Vaughn. Most of the guests were staying in the east wing of the house, but she had placed Vaughn on the west side closer to her own chambers.

There was no sign of him in the corridor, however. It was possible he was taking his repose in his bedchamber, or perhaps she had missed him on the stairs. He could be in one of the dozen other rooms in the house now, chatting with the other gentlemen. Or perhaps he had gone riding in the snow. The thought she might not see him was upsetting.

I don't want to miss him...yet I do. Then she shook her head. *I miss his kisses, that is all. I don't know the man well enough to miss him.*

She and Lysandra had discussed on more than one occasion how a man could distract a woman from her academic focuses with their passions. At the time, Perdita had no personal experience to argue with, but now...now she understood completely how a man could so thoroughly disrupt one's thoughts.

Perdita went to one of the bookcases and took out a leather portfolio containing several essays she was working on. She then settled into a little window seat in the library, her latest astronomy paper resting on her lap. She still had revisions to make, but today she wanted to read it for clarity and construction before she sent it on to Lysandra. She raised her legs up in a bent position so that her red satin slippers peeped out from the hem of her skirts, and she rested the pages on her knees.

She wasn't sure how long she'd sat there before she had the distinct impression that someone was watching her. It was far too easy to lose herself in her work, and apparently she hadn't noticed someone enter the library. The hairs on the back of her neck rose, and she tried not to panic, her first concern being that Samuel Milburn had found her alone. She raised her head and glanced about.

A lone figure leaned against the shelf not too far from where she sat in her alcove. When she saw who it was she wasn't afraid, but her heart still jerked into a rushed pace.

"Vaughn!" she hissed. "You startled me!" She set her paper aside as he came over. She tried to stand, but he prevented this by sliding onto the seat beside her.

"You were quite engrossed in whatever you were reading. I didn't wish to intrude upon your thoughts." He gently lifted her feet and stretched her legs over his lap, the position highly scandalous, but the cozy intimacy was so irresistible she didn't protest...much.

"We shouldn't..."

"Nonsense." He moved her skirts so he could place one of his large hands on her left calf.

Perdita jolted. "No, Vaughn..." She grabbed his wrist, and he lifted his face to hers.

"Easy, my sweet, just breathe." His fingers stilled on her leg, and he leaned in to brush his lips over hers. His gentle kiss calmed her, even though a rush of shivers danced along her skin.

"Better?" he asked with a smile against her lips.

She nodded. "Yes. I was just frightened."

"That's what makes passion exciting." He paused to stroke her leg again. "But I will take things as slowly as you wish."

"But I thought you liked control." She said the words softly, even though no one but the books could witness this scandalous moment.

"I do, darling. I adore control. But only once the lady feels safe with me."

"I feel safe with you," she replied truthfully.

"Good. That matters to me greatly." He continued to stroke her calf, and she closed her eyes briefly, relishing his touch.

His fingers were long and elegant but not delicate. Beautiful hands...for a handsome man. Perdita watched in fascination as his hands touched her. The heat of his palms soaked through her white stockings to her skin, and she couldn't stop the wave of heat that followed through her whole body.

A true rogue could conjure up passion like a wizard. He could cast spells that made her forsake rational thought with only a wicked smile and a tender caress from her ankle up to her knee. He let her skirts fall back down over her legs but kept his hand on her skin. There was something seductive about his hand beneath her dress, touching her legs, without being able to see what he was doing. It was as though the excitement of what he *might* do next was greater than what he actually did. She wiggled slightly but made no attempt to flee.

"Now, what were you reading that had you so enraptured?" Vaughn was gazing at her, his blue eyes clear as a summer sky. The sunlight came in through the window, trickling down his golden hair and illuminating the strands until they glowed in a halo about his head. His lips were slightly curved, as though he was lost in a pleasant but possibly scandalous daydream. It was the sort of expression a woman could stare at for hours and wish desperately that it was she the gentleman had upon his mind.

"Oh, I was just..." She tried to tuck the pages of her astronomy essay behind her, but he reached around her body and pulled the essay in front of him to read it.

"Please, don't—"

"Shh. I'm *reading*," he teased as he continued to stroke her left calf in tickling circles with his fingertips, then paused. "Astronomy?" he asked.

"Are you surprised that a woman might have a love of the sciences?"

"Surprised perhaps, but far from displeased. It has been my experience that far too many men lack a proper interest. They learn enough to feign knowledge at their gentlemen's clubs and pass along half-remembered conclusions as if they were their own. It can be quite depressing when one is looking for decent, intelligent conversation."

"And you? Do you have an interest in the sciences?"

"I do, though I admit that I am woefully ignorant of the more detailed elements of the subject of this piece. It seems quite brilliant." His eyes ran the length of the page as though scanning it.

"You think so?" She couldn't resist wanting to preen at his praise.

Vaughn did not answer at first, and his brow was furrowed as he studied the pages. "Do you know the man who wrote this? His observations are quite interesting, though I daresay some of the calculations are over my head."

"Er—yes. I know the man. He's pursuing publication of the piece, once it is ready." She was not going to tell him she was the article's author. He was no doubt the sort of man who believed women did not belong in the sciences.

"I imagine he will have success then. Does he often have you read his work beforehand?"

She nodded. It didn't feel right to conceal anything from him, but this was a part of her life that held no connection to the bargain they'd made, and she would not share this secret with him. She was far too accustomed to men thinking ill of women who had minds of their own, and did not need his ridicule whilst they were trying to keep up their engagement act. "Where were you this morning? I thought you might come down for breakfast."

Vaughn smiled his infuriating cat-in-the-cream grin. "A man ought to have a few mysteries about him." He moved his hand beneath her skirts again, this time even higher, until he touched the soft garter that held the stocking up. He flicked the silk ribbon bows, and another wave of heat rolled through her.

"Would you like me to teach you about passion?" he asked, his voice now velvety soft.

Despite her body's cries of yes, she shook her head. "No, thank you, I'm well versed in it."

He grinned, still toying with the bow of her garter. "Liar. You're afraid to risk it."

"I most certainly am not," she huffed, then curiosity got the better of her. "Risk what, exactly?"

"Falling in love with me, of course." His crooked grin should not have made her heart flutter, but it did.

"I see no danger of that, I assure you." She took the papers from him and climbed off her seat. She set her article on a nearby table and went toward the nearest bookshelf. There were three rows of shelves that were parallel to the door, and she often liked to hide behind the last one to go unseen if someone came to the library looking for her.

Perdita glanced over her shoulder and saw Vaughn following her. He trailed his fingertips along the surface of the walnut reading table. The burgundy waistcoat he wore went well with his dark-tan trousers. Perdita had to jerk her thoughts away from how well-fitted those trousers were.

"So...you say you know of passion, that you are well versed in it, but I assure you, you don't know what it means to be with *me*." He said this softly as he came up behind her. She faced the shelves, hidden from the rest of the library. Vaughn toyed with the flare of her skirts at her lower back, tugging on a red silk ribbon that trailed down her back from the sash at her waist.

"This is not part of our arrangement," she said at last, though less defiantly than she had intended.

"You misunderstand me. What I'm trying to say is that whenever Milburn sees us together, he needs to *believe* we are lovers." He leaned against her from behind, cornering her against the shelf. His lips feathered against her ear, and she shivered. Her womb clenched, and her knees ached.

"He will believe," she replied, though her words trembled.

"I have no doubts that you are a fine actress, but I fear that without some experience you will do no better than a young girl swooning over her first infatuation. Milburn will see it for what it is—drawing attention to itself and utterly unconvincing."

"And what would you suggest?"

"That you let go of your fears and allow me to guide you on a short voyage into those passions, while keeping your greater virtue intact. Only then will you be able to tap into those thoughts in Milburn's presence. Only then will he see in your eyes what you want him to see."

Perdita huffed. "I am sure you would say anything to get under a woman's skirts."

"True, I would. But it does not make my words any less reasonable."

Her eyes narrowed, but she relented. "I have found your kisses a pleasant enough diversion. I doubt whatever it is you have in mind will be much different." She threw out the challenge, and then her heart raced to see what he would do.

"And that, my dear, shows how much you have to learn." The heat of his body pressed against hers made her forget for a moment how to breathe.

"So you would teach me, then?" She kept her tone light, even though she was feeling strangely light-headed.

"Teach you to be wicked? Absolutely," Vaughn said. "When you sit across from me at dinner and I look at you, he will see in your eyes and through the blush of your cheeks that we spent an hour in the library together, doing *this*..." He lifted her skirts, traced his hand up her right leg beneath her petticoats, and touched her *there*.

Perdita gasped, but he covered her mouth with his other hand. Rather than be frightened that he was silencing her, she was excited by the way he took control. She clutched the shelf in front of her, a wet heat pooling between her thighs as he explored her with his fingers.

"He should see that I own you, that I have touched you here and tortured you until you were begging for sweet release." He murmured each wicked thought in her ear, and she struggled to stay standing. She wasn't afraid, not of his muffling her sounds or the gentle but firm exploration of her folds with his fingers. He knew just how to touch her, how to stroke her. She had never known being touched in such a way could feel so...*wild*. The rush of sensations below her waist, the way her nipples hardened against her corset, his warm breath against her neck, all mixed with the press of his body against hers from behind...it was too much.

"Show me your dark side, Perdita," Vaughn whispered, and she felt her body seize and come apart. Stars dotted her vision, and she felt herself falling. Strong arms caught her, lifting her back up.

She realized through the haze of her slowly dissipating climax that he was carrying her away from the bookshelves and back to the window seat. She blinked against the bright sunlight as he set her back down on the window seat's soft cushions. Her head was swimming with a thousand emotions, but most of her felt dazed, shaky, and confused. He had just touched her at the apex of her thighs, and she'd come undone. The sensations, the heated explosion inside her was like nothing she'd ever felt before.

She looked up at him, blinking as she tried to stay calm and not cry. What he'd done had her feeling open and vulnerable. She wanted him to hold her, keep her close while she came down from the steep height her body had climbed. He leaned over and brushed his lips over hers.

"Tonight at dinner, when I look at you, think of this moment, my hands on your bare skin between your pretty thighs. Milburn will see what you wish him to see."

With that he turned and walked away, leaving Perdita bewildered, her body lax yet trembling on a floating cloud of feelings she was too afraid to analyze. Vaughn was a *master* of sin, there was no doubt. She couldn't help but worry that a small part of her might indeed be in danger of falling in love with him.

Perhaps he was truly more dangerous to her than Samuel.

VAUGHN RAPPED HIS KNUCKLES ON THE DOOR TO MR. DARBY'S study.

"Come in."

Vaughn entered and found Darby bent over his desk examining a collection of shells with a magnifying glass. Snow fell outside the bay window behind him, which would leave a fresh layer for any gentleman riding tomorrow.

Vaughn's impression of Darby was that he was a rather studious man, a man invested in the sciences. Just like his daughter, it would seem. He suspected she'd written that essay she'd been reviewing and she had tried to hide the fact from him. But her expression had given her away. Her face had been so open, her eyes so earnest in that moment as she seemed to yearn for his approval.

No doubt she was afraid he would be just like any other man and discount her ideas. But her arguments were sound and her conclusions logical. It was a paper worthy of publication, regardless of who had written it. He would find a way to convince her of that once they were married.

"Ah, Lord Darlington. I've been expecting you." Darby chuckled as he set the magnifying glass down.

"Well, I wasn't sure if...your daughter had informed you."

Vaughn was in uncharted territory here. He'd never expected to be in this situation, yet here he was.

"Your engagement? She mentioned it. I was a little surprised, of course. Perdy tells me almost everything, and she's never mentioned you before, except this past September." Darby studied him with a gentle curiosity. It surprised Vaughn. Most fathers with unmarried daughters would have been chasing a man like him off their estates unless they were desperate. Yet Darby was far more like his daughter than Vaughn might have guessed. He was of a rational mind, just like her.

"I admit we should have come to you at once, but I did not want to trap her into any commitment until she was sure she wished to marry me."

Darby chuckled. "Noble words for one of London's more notorious rogues, or so I hear. You aren't part of that League of Rogues are you?"

Vaughn shook his head. "No, certainly not." The League was not simply some club one could join, though gossip spoke of them as if it was. Investing with Ashton Lennox, one of the League members, was as close as he would get to being part of their number.

"Good, good. So you're here to ask for my permission to marry Perdita?"

He nodded.

"Well, as you know, my daughter has her own heart and mind. My opinion on the matter holds little weight. She will do exactly as she pleases."

"That may be true," Vaughn replied, "but I also believe she values your opinion. I feel duty bound to pass any test you might put me through so that she will feel you accept the match as well."

Darby tilted his head. "Are you aware that another gentleman here at the house has expressed an interest in Perdita's hand?"

"Samuel Milburn? Yes, I'm aware, although he has no idea of our engagement. We were hoping to have you announce our happy news tonight at dinner. We believe it might direct the other fellow to seek another bride." Vaughn knew full well that it would be hard to prevent Milburn from pursuing his blackmail on Perdita, but he secretly hoped that once Milburn saw that Vaughn was in fact going to marry her—assuming he could convince her it was a sound idea—that Milburn would give up.

"I see."

Vaughn waited, but Darby didn't speak further.

"You will make the announcement?" he prompted.

Rather than answer Vaughn, the older man stroked his chin, studying Vaughn as though he were a shell beneath his magnifying glass.

"*Why* do you want to marry my daughter? I'm aware of your financial troubles, but there are many heiresses worth far more that I'm sure you could easily win over. What makes my Perdita of such interest to you?"

That was the test he had been expecting. He had to answer carefully but also honestly. Darby had the look about him of a man who could read a person well. Vaughn reached for a conch shell and examined it.

"What makes this conch shell worth studying more than the rest tucked away on your shelves? The color of this shell and the exquisite pattern of its grooves make it unique among the rest. Perdita isn't like other ladies I've met. She's genuine. She challenges me without fear, and I find that engaging. She's a damned clever creature too. Did you know she's pursuing publication of her scholarly articles on astronomy? She told me she was reading them over for some gentleman, but the handwriting is too clear and neat to belong to a man. I recognized it at once as hers. Her conclusions are brilliant, and I plan to do everything in my power to assist in her pursuits." He smiled at the thought. "Watching her show up those old fellows at the astronomy society would be quite satisfying." Vaughn paused when he realized he'd been gushing over Perdita like a young boy.

Mr. Darby watched him with open amusement. "Glad to see your affections are well placed. But I won't offer my blessings until you *prove* your love. She can marry you or not as she chooses, but know that I have my eye on you, Darlington. Break her heart and I'll bury you in my woods where no one will ever find you."

The threat, though pleasantly delivered, had been unexpected. Darby cared deeply about his daughter. It would have made the older man proud to know his daughter protected him just as fiercely, but as Perdita had made no mention of the blackmail to her father, Vaughn would follow her lead and maintain his silence on the matter.

"Understood."

"Good. Now, why don't you help the other young lads collect the Yule log. We must light it tonight."

"Of course." Vaughn left Darby in the study and asked a passing footman to have his cloak, hat, and gloves brought to him. When he reached the front door, he found a crowd of young men already there, all dressed warmly. They were chatting away and laughing as they readied themselves for the Yule log-gathering party.

"Are you joining them?"

Perdita suddenly appeared at his side. Lord, the woman could be stealthy. Once they were married, he would have to have little bells sewn onto her gown so he could hear her coming.

"I was instructed by your father to assist the others." He took his cloak from the footman who had rushed to him with his outerwear.

"You listened to my father? Goodness, Lord Darlington, whatever reasonable, gentlemanly thing shall you do next? I swear you'll lose your wicked reputation at this rate," she teased him, and he adored the sparkle in her eyes as she did.

"As a *gentleman*"—he emphasized the word—"I would like to invite you to join us."

Her winged brows rose. "Truly? Most men would not think to invite a woman to partake in such a sacred and masculine ritual."

Vaughn glanced at the collection of eager young lads surrounding them and sighed dramatically.

"Miss Darby, please do me the honor of saving me from this hoard of bucks, who will surely drive me to the nearest bottle with their inane antics if I do not have a grounded, sensible creature to accompany me."

She giggled. "In that case, I accept. Let me fetch my cloak and gloves."

He couldn't deny the excitement that fluttered in him at the thought of spending more time with her. When he'd come upon her in the library earlier, she'd stopped him dead. Before, he'd always focused on women most when they were naked in his bed, but there was something different about Perdita. She was fiery, challenging, yet alluring and sweet. He hadn't known a woman could be so complex in personality. He found he rather liked that depth to her.

When he'd spied her in the library window seat, he had known he would find a way to rouse her passions, but he hadn't expected to be so affected by her reactions to him. Holding her in the library, thinking of her secretly penning astronomy essays and defying the conventions of society, then picturing the way she blushed at his exploring hands before trusting him to bring her to climax...something inside him clicked into place.

This plan of a false engagement had begun as a way to climb out of financial ruin, but everything had changed, and that no longer mattered. What mattered now was winning her heart and claiming her as his wife. He knew he'd settle for no other woman. She was a bottomless pool of mysteries, an enchantress who drew him out with her innocent lips and eyes full of secrets. He was quite convinced he could spend years getting to know who Perdita really was.

Vaughn was still picturing how she tasted when he noticed Samuel Milburn staring at him from across the hall. The man was scowling.

Milburn nodded. "Darlington."

Vaughn ignored the sour look he was given and offered a nod

back. Then Milburn came over, dodging the other young men as they bounded about the hall like pups.

"Chasing the skirts of Miss Darby, are we?" he asked.

"Chasing? No. *Caught*." He smiled slowly, watching his meaning sink in for the other man.

"Caught? By that you mean..."

"We are engaged. The announcement is to be made tonight at dinner." Vaughn pulled on his gloves, allowing his usual uncaring manner to be displayed. He didn't want Milburn to see any desperation or urgency. The man must not sense the true purpose of their engagement.

Milburn's cheeks reddened, and his eyes narrowed. "When did you court her? She's been in the country for the last few months, and I know you've been visiting the gaming dens in London."

Milburn was too bloody astute for his own good. Vaughn finished with his gloves and arched a brow. "You can't expect a gentleman to reveal his secrets." Let the bastard make what he could of that.

"I had intentions toward her myself. I'd already spoken to Darby." Milburn's voice turned into a low, warning growl. That would have bothered some gentlemen, especially those who knew of Milburn's cruel and abusive nature. But Vaughn wasn't one of them.

"Sorry to tell you that I got there first, old boy. And you know I have no intention of sharing what's mine with any man." Vaughn slapped the other man on the shoulder. He felt the tension rise between them. They weren't foolish young lads barely out of the schoolroom. They were men, ready to face each other down like stags over territory. Vaughn was more than ready to battle the bastard for Perdita's sake. He'd love a chance to bloody his knuckles on Milburn's face.

Milburn seemed ready to argue further, but Perdita appeared at the top of the stairs, wearing a red cloak with white ermine fur lining the edges. Her dark hair had escaped the loosely pulled up Grecian style, and bright-red ribbons had been threaded into her hair to hold back her locks. She was a perfectly delectable little creature.

And she's all mine.

Vaughn grinned eagerly as she came down the stairs, and he held out his hands to her. She placed her gloved hands in his, allowing him a moment to study her. She had a cloak on, but her gown seemed a bit thin for walking about in the woods.

"Will you be warm enough, darling?" he asked, genuinely concerned. One did not charge about the snowy woods in a fine tea gown.

"Yes. This isn't my best gown, but I didn't want to miss out on the experience simply because I had to change my dress." When her nose wrinkled, it made her adorably sweet, and Vaughn couldn't resist smiling. Damn, since when had such sweetness ever been so fetching to him? His bed partners before had been moody, sensual, and as friendly as cats in heat, but Perdita was nothing like them, and he found that refreshing. She turned as though just now realizing Milburn was standing there next to them.

"Oh, my apologies, Mr. Milburn. Did I interrupt your conversation?" Her wide eyes were filled with innocence, but Vaughn knew she had interrupted them on purpose and was glad for it.

Vaughn answered for him. "No, you did not. We were simply catching up, weren't we, Milburn?" He challenged his rival with one lazy and somewhat contemptuous look.

Milburn's dark eyes burned with a hateful fire, but he couldn't lose his temper in front of the other guests. He stormed off, shoving a few lads out of his way viciously enough to have them grumbling and brushing their coats in displeasure.

"No holiday spirit there," said one.

Vaughn turned to his fiancée. "My, that was exciting. A bit like poking an angry bear." He chuckled and offered Perdita his arm.

It seemed the others had decided they were ready to begin, and the crowd of men suddenly rushed out the front door in a wall of fluttering cloaks and clattering boots. They bounded into the snow like hearty young foxhounds.

Perdita giggled as the men began their wild romp toward the forest that bordered the property. "Heavens, look at them go. You'd think they'd been kept indoors for a week."

"My lady." Vaughn lifted her by the waist and set her down in the snow. Some of the men had already worn down a steadier path ahead of them. It would be much easier on her skirts to walk on packed snow.

Perdita turned her head to hide a blush, then lifted her gown with one hand and began to walk. Vaughn took her other arm, and they moved together into the woods. Due to the heavy snowfall, only a few birds were chattering on trees, and Vaughn couldn't resist the temptation to tease Perdita.

"Look there." He pointed with his free hand toward a blue-and-yellow bird with black markings around its throat and eyes. It clung agilely to a tiny bare branch of a stout little tree.

"Oh, he's lovely." Perdita paused to watch the bird. The branch was thin enough that the bird's weight made it dip and bounce as the creature adjusted its position and fluttered its wings.

"That is a blue tit," he said. "Tits always turn blue in the winter when it's cold. He has a cousin called a great tit, similar markings, but a much bigger chap." He waited, holding his breath to see if she realized the joke he was trying to make, that the tits which turned blue weren't birds...

"I believe you're trying to tease me."

"Whatever do you mean?"

"You know as well as I do that tit has *other* meanings."

"As far as I know it simply refers to a diminutive creature, such as a titmouse or a tomtit. I cannot be responsible for any meanings *your* imagination has come up with."

"Well, nevertheless, you must stop talking about *blue tits*," she whispered in a half-amused, half-scandalized tone.

"I promise to return yours to a lovely shade of pink once we get back inside."

"Vaughn!" she admonished.

"What? You began such talk, but that doesn't mean I cannot

contribute. Yes, I believe a few kisses, a bit of sucking will bring the pink back nicely." He leaned down to murmur the last part, which only made her gasp.

"Stop this," Perdita said, her face already beginning to flush.

"I suppose you don't want to hear me describe chaffinches? They have the most attractive pink breasts."

She looked as if she might punch him, but then she thought better of it. She huffed and walked a few steps ahead before she bent down. Before he realized what she was up to, he caught a face full of snow.

He brushed off the powdery residue from his face, sputtering.

"You will pay for that, my darling." He crouched down and started to collect his own handful of snow in his gloves. When he rose, ready to aim, there was no sign of her.

But he saw a clear track of dainty boot prints in the snow, leading deeper into the woods. With a wolfish grin, he began to stalk his lady, looking for signs of a red cloak within the snowy forest. When he caught his red-hooded lady, she would pay for her mischievous behavior, and they would both enjoy every minute of it.

CHAPTER 6

P erdita wrapped the edges of her cloak tightly about her body to keep it from showing around the base of the large tree she hid behind. Throwing a snowball at Vaughn had been far too great a temptation to resist. She liked to see him ruffled and caught off guard. He seemed more real and a little less like the rogue from a schoolgirl's forbidden daydreams. Not that she minded that side of him, but she longed to see the real Vaughn, not the façade he showed to the rest of the world.

Once she'd thrown that snowball, she knew he would seek revenge, no doubt in a wicked way that would leave her breathless and shaky. So she'd turned tail and fled to make the chase much more rewarding for them both.

She should have chosen her white cloak rather than the red, but she had so loved the contrast of red against the snow.

AND NOW I SHALL PAY FOR IT.

Far ahead of her, she could see the young men in their quest for the perfect Yule log. They needed something large that would burn for twelve days. It wasn't really possible to find a log that large, but men loved to challenge each other over silly things like that.

Perdita turned her focus back to the forest. She closed her eyes, taking in the sounds around her. The chatter of the blue tits and the occasional snap and creak of frozen branches were the only noises she could detect. She opened her eyes, wondering where Vaughn had gone, or if he had moved at all. As she peered around the tree, she almost expected to see him close by, ready to pounce. Nothing. The forest was empty as far back as the path that led to the house.

Where the devil had he gone? She turned back to the woods and screamed. Vaughn had somehow gotten around her! Her heart leapt into her throat at the sudden unexpected sight. He pushed her flat against the tree and clamped one gloved hand over her mouth.

"You left your delectable behind unguarded, sweeting." The *tsk* he gave was gentle and wicked, just as his smile was in that moment. He pressed his body against hers, his hips against her stomach. She'd never felt so small and vulnerable as she did at that moment. It should have scared her. Any young lady in a similar position would have been terrified, but Vaughn holding her captive like a dark winter forest god set fire to her blood.

I am as wicked as he is. The realization was buried beneath a rush of sensations as Vaughn removed his hand from her mouth and kissed her. It was a ruthless sort of kiss, one that marked her, conquered her, and reminded her that she belonged to him—yet not in the way a man like Milburn would. Vaughn didn't own her, and he certainly didn't want to break her. But in this forest, surrounded by the snow and the silence, he owned her very soul for briefest heartbeat of a stolen kiss.

"You are clever," he whispered in her ear. "But not quick enough, I'm afraid. Shall I punish you here?" He swept one hand beneath her cloak to cup her bottom. Her body burned at the touch, even as she wondered what sort of punishment he might inflict.

"Please, Vaughn," she murmured, not sure what she was pleading for. She placed her gloved hands on his shoulders and dug her fingers in, holding on to him. He tilted her head up by placing his fingers under her chin.

"Oh, the things I could do to you..." His eyes raked over her before settling on her lips. "But I believe a kiss is what you deserve." He removed his hand from beneath her chin and bit the tips of his gloved fingers, tugging the leather off his skin. He let the glove fall into the snow beside them.

"Yes, please kiss me." Her gaze fixed on his mouth as she encouraged him. He had the most perfect lips, ones that were soft, warm, and sensual. The kind that drifted along her bare skin and melded with her own lips and seemed to erase the world around them until nothing else existed.

"Lift your skirts," he growled in a dark and demanding tone.

She shivered and whispered back, "What? Why?"

Vaughn arched a brow in a way that she was coming to recognize—that she was treading on dangerous ground by questioning him. A lady who asked him to explain his seductions might end up with more than she expected. Vaughn had mentioned spanking once before. The idea had startled her at first, but his idea of a love pat was not one of cruelty or abuse but of pleasure. The thrill of thinking of him smacking his hand lightly on her bottom was undeniably erotic, and she wanted to experience it.

"Lift them now and ask me to kiss you, darling." His voice was now low and smooth. "If you do it properly, I'll reward you. Fail and I will punish your darling little bottom. I don't care if I must bend you over my lap in the snow for all to see."

Her heart hammered while she glanced around, afraid someone would see them. "But..."

His hand caught her chin, making her focus on him again. "No one will see us, darling. The men are too far off." He swung his cloak over her left side, shielding her from anyone who might see them from that direction. "Now, raise your skirts and ask me for a kiss. And when you do, you will call me *my lord*."

The confident set of his body as he moved back, giving her room to raise her skirts, was almost as infuriating as it was exciting. Perdita clutched her skirts and hiked them up, revealing her underpinnings. The cold air hit her legs and made her shiver.

"Please kiss me..." She hesitated, and her lashes lowered for a moment, but only a moment. "My lord."

"Impertinent little creature. But that will do, for now." His condescending tone made her bristle.

But she didn't have time to reply. He swooped down on her, capturing her mouth in his. She nearly dropped her skirts, but his bare hand was suddenly between her thighs. He didn't slip his fingers into her, not like he had in the library. He only touched the sensitive nub at the top of her mound. He pressed on it, then moved the pad of his finger in small circles over it.

She shivered and tried to wriggle away. It was too sensitive, made worse in the outdoor chill, but he gripped her throat with his other hand—not squeezing but holding her still in a gentle but possessive grip. She was a prisoner of his delicious torment. Arching her back, Perdita knew she had to surrender to him, and in that moment she *wanted* to.

His tongue traced the fullness of her lips as she kissed him back hungrily. His mouth was urgent, exploring and demanding. It was everything she loved about him.

The realization sent a jolt of sensations down her body to meet his fingertips between her thighs. She wanted to belong to him, to be the only woman who ever knew his dark side, one that matched her own.

We are twin souls curled around one another, always straining for that next kiss, that next lingering caress stolen at the right moment.

Her body shook as pleasure rolled through her. She leaned back against the tree, Vaughn's cloak shielding her as the ripples of pleasure continued to flow through her. He teased her a few seconds more before he withdrew his hand and let her skirts fall back into place. He pulled his lips away from hers. They were close in body, but in that moment, she felt there was no distance between them at all. They could have been one being, one beating heart and soul.

When Vaughn's lips curved into a smile this time, there was no wickedness to it, only a boyish delight. Her heart turned over at the sight. The cool intensity of his gaze was gone. She was seeing that secret part of him she'd longed for. It was as though she'd wandered into an old attic and come upon a portrait covered in old curtains. She'd pulled away the faded fabric, and as the dust cleared, sunlight from a high window illuminated the hidden face painted in oil just for her.

It was her own private moment, one she would never have to share with the rest of the world. A piece of him that belonged to her, if only at this moment in her memory. The dreamy intimacy of it held them both spellbound.

Vaughn leaned in slowly this time, and his next kiss was sweet, soft, yet deep. His lips lingered and coaxed hers into a slow, playful dance that seemed to go on forever. She twined her arms around him, caressing the back of his neck, making him tremble when she reached a sensitive spot where his neck met his shoulders.

"What in the blazes are you doing to me?" he murmured. The confusion in his voice was soft and sweet, making her smile against his mouth.

"*Me?* It is *you* who has me bewitched," she responded.

"Then we are both under some sort of spell." He brushed his gloved hand over her cheek before he dropped his cloak from her body and bent to pick up his discarded glove. She had to let go of him, and her arms felt empty without him.

Vaughn cleared his throat. "We should catch up with the others before we are missed." He put his glove back on and then held out his hand to her. She took it, and they began the long walk into the woods to find the other men.

The rest of the party was deep into the woods by the time they found them. They had discovered a log they all agreed would be perfect as the Yule log.

"Ho there, Darlington. Care to give the beast a good whack? We're just about through." One of the young men held up a sizable ax and pointed its blade at the fallen log.

"I suppose." Vaughn removed his cloak and tossed it at the young man before he claimed the ax.

Perdita stepped back, as did the others, giving Vaughn room enough to swing.

He wielded the ax as though he'd been a woodsman to some ancient medieval queen. The silver blade arced through the air and sank into the wood with a heavy *thunk!* The trunk broke in four hard swings, and he moved four feet down its length to separate it again from the ragged base next to the stump.

"Is that enough, do you think?" he asked.

"I believe so," one of the men replied. Four others bent to lift the Yule log and begin the burdensome process of carrying it home. Vaughn went to retrieve his cloak, and another young man engaged him in conversation.

Perdita wished to join him, but such an intrusion might seem rude.

"So, you and Darlington are engaged?" Milburn's cold voice made Perdita jolt. He caught her from behind by the arm, squeezing hard, and she was rooted to the ground with him holding her in front of him, her arm twisted behind her back. If he twisted it much farther, it would break. Pain radiated up from her elbow, and she bit her bottom lip to keep from crying out.

"Unhand me. You're hurting me," she hissed.

Milburn ignored her. "I spent *four months* playing friends with that old fool you call your father, and now you accept another man in your bed? I will not stand for this. Don't forget what I told you. I can turn over my evidence to the magistrate anytime I wish. If I do, he'll be facing imprisonment or worse."

Perdita's tongue seemed to swell, and her throat choked with fear. "I haven't forgotten."

"Then I suggest you come to your senses and tell Darlington to break it off. Otherwise, your father will pay for your stubbornness."

Milburn's threat was so different from Vaughn's. Vaughn had punished her with kisses and with pleasure. Milburn was a coward and a cruel beast who simply wanted to control her every action. Despite her fear, rage came roaring to the surface. She had to fight him. If he won now, like this, she'd never be free.

"Unhand me now or I will scream. Then you will be forced to explain to these gentlemen here what you were doing." She spun to face him, her hood falling off her head. "You may frighten every other woman in London, but *not* me."

She jerked her arm free of his startled grasp, and then she leaned close. "I could not break my engagement with him even if I wished to." It was a lie, but she hoped Milburn would believe it. "Lord Darlington won't give me up, not for anything. If you harm me or my family, you will face his wrath. Never forget that," she hissed. "Speak to me like that again, and I will have you chased off my property by the dogs until your feet are sore and blistered." She kept a steady stare at him, the way one would at a dangerous animal, before she turned and strode off.

POLITENESS BE DAMNED—SHE WAS GOING TO JOIN VAUGHN. HER

temper had only just covered the swell of fear inside her at Milburn's actions. To grab her and threaten her like that? He was bolder in his intentions than she ever could've guessed, and far more dangerous than she'd wanted to believe.

She had hoped her false engagement to Vaughn would deter him. That clearly wasn't the case. She hadn't overestimated Vaughn, but she *had* underestimated Milburn. He wasn't afraid to use his supposed evidence to destroy her father. What was she going to do? She tried to convince herself that his actions were only because the wound to his pride was still fresh. Perhaps in time he would lose interest. This plan had to work, or else everything would fall apart.

Vaughn turned at her approach, his mask of cool aloofness on his handsome face.

"Miss Darby." He bent his head in polite greeting, and the other gentleman did the same. "Is everything all right?"

She painted a false smile on her lips. "Yes." She knew if she told Vaughn what had happened, he might use the ax he still held to chop Milburn into pieces. As appealing as the idea was right then, she couldn't allow that to happen.

"Are you cold? I offer myself as an escort back to the house." He provided his arm gallantly in front of the other men.

She nodded and slipped her arm through his. "Thank you." He handed the ax back to the others, and they started to walk back. Milburn was nowhere to be seen at first, but then she spied him a dozen yards away, talking to his companion. It didn't reassure her. She had a terrible feeling that Samuel Milburn was not going to back down.

CHAPTER 7

Vaughn lounged against the wall at the back of the large drawing room which was already full of gentlemen in their evening clothes. He did not feel like joining in their conversations at the moment. The ladies had been coming down in pairs for the last hour before dinner, but there was no sign of Perdita.

He didn't like it. She wasn't the sort of woman who took overly long preparing herself for dinner. Guilt gnawed at him. He worried that what he'd done in the woods had been a step too far. She had been pale and withdrawn on the journey back, and he hadn't been able to coax her out of her thoughts, even to tell him more about her love of science. He'd even teased her about the names of constellations, pronouncing them wrong, but she hadn't corrected him.

The distant look in her eyes had eaten away at his confidence. He'd never worried about his actions with a woman before, but with Perdita *everything* he did mattered.

Did I push too much? Demand something she couldn't give? Most gently bred ladies did not enjoy his particular flavor of passion— the commands, the obedience, the edge of pain blurring into pleasure. It was why he never seduced innocents and kept his activities restricted to widows and mistresses who shared his hungers.

When he'd kissed Perdita today in the woods, she'd surrendered *so sweetly* and had turned his world on its axis, shifting everything like tumbling sands in an hourglass. He was still unsettled at how perfect she was, how much it had tested his self-control not to take her there and then. But perhaps he had seen only what he wanted to see. Perhaps she had been afraid of him and not truly interested in him.

Was he so starved for a woman's touch that he'd misread her? Was she even now hiding from him because she was too ashamed of what had happened, afraid he would do it again? He couldn't bear the thought. He wouldn't forgive himself if it turned out he'd had it all wrong. But before he could seek her out to apologize, the door opened at the far end of the room and Perdita appeared.

She wore a ruby-red silk gown with a flounced hem trimmed in white lace, as though snowflakes had been caught on the lush fabric. Her bodice was embroidered with tiny flowers, and puffed sleeves clung to her elegantly sloping shoulders. A few loose dark curls bounced and caressed her creamy skin. Skin that he longed to taste. The woman was a vision of loveliness, and he feared he had ruined any chance of marrying her.

He held his breath, pacing around the room's edge toward her, watching her as she spoke to other guests. He studied every tilt of her head, every move, trying to figure out what was going on in her head. His blood burned at the thought of her, but fear held him back. At last he decided to speak to her. Perhaps her tone toward him would reveal more.

Perdita's father stepped in between him and his goal. "Darlington."

He met the older man's amused face with smothered frustration. He needed to speak to Perdita, to ask if she was all right. The last person he wanted to speak to was her father, a man who would most likely shoot him if he knew what Vaughn had been up to with his daughter.

"Yes?"

"I have spoken to Perdita, and she's agreed that making the announcement tonight will be fine. I thought I would make a toast during dinner. Does that suit you?"

"You spoke to her?" Vaughn hung on that single fact, his heart racing. "When?"

Darby tilted his head. "After you returned with the Yule log. I trust things haven't changed since we spoke this afternoon?"

"No, certainly not. I am just glad to hear she spoke to you." It gave him a glimmer of hope that perhaps she had enjoyed their time in the woods and that he hadn't frightened her off. Still, she could just as easily be continuing with her plans to dissuade Milburn's pursuit.

"She did." Darby's eyes held a twinkle. "I admit, I didn't believe it until she told me how fond she was of you. I won't deny my daughter her heart's desire, but"—he leaned in close to Vaughn—"my threat about burying you still stands. You'd best not break her heart, or they will never find you."

Vaughan nodded slowly in understanding.

"Good." Darby smacked his shoulder with an open palm and stepped out of his way.

Perdita was alone now, watching him. He could feel the eyes of the room, particularly those of the ladies, tracking him as he and Perdita met. They would whisper behind their fans about this meeting, speculate on every look, every smile or word shared between them. He couldn't stop them, nor would he try. That was the entire point of this charade—for people to talk, to notice that they were together, and for word of it to reach Milburn over and over until he lost hope of his pursuit.

For a moment, neither of them spoke. She opened her lips, and he found himself afraid of what she might say. He rushed to speak before her. "About today...in the woods." He looked for any sign of horror at the reminder of that moment. "I didn't... I shouldn't have made you do that."

Perdita's lips parted even farther, and her eyes widened. "But..."

She leaned in closer. "I *liked* what we did." She frowned. "Did it not satisfy you?" She raised a gloved hand to her lips, her cheeks pinkening with a sudden blush.

"No!" He reached out to grasp her other hand. "That is to say," he clarified at her wounded expression, "I did enjoy it. Too much. I feared I'd frightened you, that you'd seen my black heart and it was too much for you." He faltered when he realized he was confessing to such wild things. Things that no man should say to a woman. He sounded like Vaughn's friend Ambrose. That fool had rushed headlong into love for Perdita's friend and never looked back. Vaughn had no intention of falling in love, even with his future wife. He'd always wished to have an affection for his wife, because it would make a marriage happier, but love was too dangerous, too volatile an emotion. He never wanted to risk his black heart for love.

Rather than rush to reassure him or deny that she had been afraid, Perdita raised her chin. Her warm brown eyes seemed to glow with some mixture of amusement and elation.

"Vaughn, if you had tried to do anything to me that I did not wish, I wouldn't have let you." Her lips curved into a ghost of a smile, and the wit and confidence he'd feared had left her was back.

Still, he could not resist asking. "But when we came back, you were so quiet. I was worried—"

"The infamous rogue worries over me?" She was still smiling, but for a brief instant, he saw that shadow in her eyes. Then it was gone. "I admit my thoughts were elsewhere," she said. "But it had nothing to do with you or what transpired between us."

The flood of relief at her words was surprising. He hadn't known until that moment just how much he needed her to tell him she was all right.

"Now, I'm afraid we shan't be sitting close at dinner. Mother has spread us out in the seating arrangements." Her nose wrinkled as she showed her clear distaste for this arrangement.

"She didn't put you near..." He gave a slight jerk of his head toward Millburn.

"No, thank heavens." Perdita's eyes brightened again. "After dinner, I thought we might talk. We must prepare for him seeing us together, correct? One in private?" Her gaze dropped to his lips, and he could guess what she was truly thinking. The excited gleam in her eyes was impossible to miss. The little minx clearly missed him and all the wicked things he could do. *And to think I was concerned she didn't enjoy it.*

She bit her lip. "Oh dear, you're grinning again."

"Hmm?" He realized she was right, but he couldn't stop.

"You worry me when you look like that. Like a wolf looking at a rather plump rabbit."

His smile widened. "I do like my rabbits plump." He offered her a playful smirk and won a heated blush from her.

The door to the drawing room opened, and dinner was announced. Vaughn tucked her arm in his with a chuckle.

He leaned down to whisper in her ear. "Remember our time in the library. Whenever I drink from my goblet of wine, I shall be thinking about how you taste." He felt a shiver ripple through her. *That* would keep her occupied this evening, because he planned to drink a lot of wine.

The couples convened in the dining room, their voices bouncing through the corridors. Darby House seemed to always be a place of life and delight, no matter the time of year. The gold lamplight glowing on the shimmering evening gowns painted a pretty picture amidst the fine furnishings. There was a lively elegance to it all that spoke of money spent, but spent well. It was nothing like his parents and how they would have run the home.

When his older brother, Edward, had died, the loss had broken his parents' spirits. They had never been deeply in love as a married couple, but they had shared a love for their eldest son that bound them together in grief. Vaughn hadn't been given much thought before his brother's death, and after his passing he became only a forced interest. His father had retreated to his club, and the debts soon began to mount, while his mother withered away day by day, sometimes spending hours in Edward's room, clutching a miniature portrait to her breast.

The servants moved like ghosts in the gloomy, quiet house, and Vaughn had no strength in him to fight his parents' plans to turn their home into a mausoleum for their dead son. Instead, he'd obtained a bachelor's residence on Jermyn Street and stayed there until they died. It had left him with a bittersweet ache for the beauty and the warmth he felt here at Darby House. His desire to secretly win Perdita's hand was growing, but he now doubted his ability to give her a warm and happy life she deserved. He hadn't been raised by sensible, loving parents like she had, and he wouldn't know the first thing about making a life like that for her.

"Now *you* are frowning," Perdita teased, mimicking his scowl.

He couldn't resist a gentle laugh. "I am. Deep thoughts always make me frown." He buried his dark thoughts and added in a low whisper, "I think we should meet tonight. The library after midnight?"

"Agreed," she answered back, just as quietly.

They entered the dining room, and there was no more opportunity to speak privately. Vaughn escorted Perdita to her seat at the far end of the table before he walked back to his own. He was seated near Perdita's mother.

Damnation. He couldn't see Perdita's face, the various decorations on the table blocked his view. A large stuffed pheasant's colorful feathers flared out as though it was ready to take flight. Vaughn could just see the curve of Perdita's neck through the dip of the back of the bird's wings.

Dinner wasn't going to be as enjoyable as he had hoped. He looked toward the elderly gentleman who sat to his left. He had a better view of Perdita.

He nudged the older fellow. "Excuse me. Would you mind trading places with me?"

The old man's face turned ruddy as his eyes darted quickly to Mrs. Darby and back to him. "Trade places?" he blustered. "Good

God, man, the lady of the house is right there beside you. The sanctity of a lady's table seating is the cornerstone of our empire!" He announced this so loudly it drew surprised gazes from the ladies and gentlemen nearby. Even Perdita was staring at him, worry creasing her brow.

Vaughn rubbed a hand over his face and sighed. *Cornerstone of the empire? For God's sake.* There was nothing like public mortification in the middle of a Christmas dinner to shame even a hardened rogue like himself. He was half tempted to find the nearest Christmas pudding and shove his face into it to avoid the stares. The elderly man was still watching him.

"What the devil would make you demand to swap seats, young man?"

Vaughn almost choked. *Young man?* He hadn't been called that in years. Hadn't *felt* like that in years. He was twenty-seven, not some boy fresh out of school. He cleared his throat.

"I merely hoped to have a better view of a certain young lady." Damn, why did he feel flushed all of a sudden?

"A lady, you say?" The old man lowered his voice and leaned in conspiratorially. "Empire be damned." He poked Vaughn. "Out of your chair, boy."

Vaughn glanced toward Mrs. Darby, seeking her approval.

"I'll allow it," Mrs. Darby said. She smiled a knowing little smile before she turned to the guest on her other side to engage him in conversation.

Vaughn hastily exited his chair and switched with the old man. When he sat down, he glanced toward Perdita. She raised one hand to cover her mouth, no doubt hiding a smile. Even from across the vast distance of the dinner table he could see that darling twinkle in her eyes, and it made him feel...*giddy*. He grinned, feeling like a damned fool, but oddly, he didn't mind. Vaughn reached for his glass of wine and took a sip. Perdita blushed, and he chuckled. Perfect.

"Nice to see young love," the old man commented. "Everyone seems to assume that when you're my age we forget what it's like to be young. You'd better hold on to her, my boy." The older man's tone turned wistful, and he tugged on his cravat.

"Oh, I'm not in love. I barely know her."

"Balderdash. Love doesn't require you *knowing* everything about her. Sometimes love is part of the mystery. Especially for men. Women will always have their secrets, the little twinkles in their eyes, the hidden smiles that make us wonder just what it is they are thinking about. My Arabella is still quite the mystery, and we've been married fifty years." He nodded toward an older woman who sat close to Perdita. Her loveliness hadn't faded with time, and Vaughn could still see the attraction.

Vaughn was tempted to argue that it wasn't really possible to love someone you didn't know, but Mr. Darby stood up with a glass in his hand, drawing everyone's attention.

"Thank you for joining my family for Christmas. It's so lovely to have guests during the holidays. It warms my heart to have my house full of people." His thanks were followed by a murmur of agreement by the guests. "And tonight, I have some wonderful news. I'm delighted to share with you all that my daughter, Perdita, and Lord Darlington are engaged. I would like to propose a toast— to Lord Darlington and my daughter, Perdita."

The guests echoed his toast and drank to it. Perdita sipped her wine, her head down, but she was red-faced. Vaughn was tempted to do the same. Everyone at the long table stared at them as the news settled in. It was one thing to be invited to Darby House for a party, but to be announced as Perdita's intended was going to cause ripples in the various social circles. He'd expected that, of course, even counted on it, but watching it occur before his eyes in a roomful of people was both embarrassing and fascinating. He wasn't sure what he ought to do, so he resorted to his usual behavior and flashed a cool smile at the curious faces turned his way.

"And finally, to remind you all," Darby said, clearing his throat, "tomorrow night, we shall have the ball." This second announce- ment did the considerate job of distracting the ladies, who all murmured in delight at the coming dance. Many of the young men in attendance grinned eagerly, and the dinner began.

Vaughn paid little attention to much else over the next two hours. His focus was on Perdita. He loved to watch her. There was something enchanting about the way her eyes lit up as she talked. She was an animated creature, but there was no falseness about her, no shallow vapidity like far too many ladies her age tended to display. She was both genuine and honest. Her words were always well chosen and truthful.

A gentleman beside her made her laugh, and Vaughn grinned at the sound. A pang of jealousy followed. He wanted to be the man who made her laugh like that.

"Someone's not happy you won the fair lady," the old man on his left muttered. His words dragged Vaughn's attention away from Perdita.

"What do you mean?"

The man nodded down the table. "That fellow at the far end. He looks quite put out. Did you steal his sweetheart, I wonder?"

Of course it was Samuel Milburn who was glowering at him, his black eyes filled with rage, his mouth a thin line. Vaughn had been so focused on Perdita that he'd forgotten the whole reason he was here: to save her from that bastard.

"Actually, I didn't steal her. I rescued her," Vaughn responded truthfully.

"Did you, now?" The old man chuckled before he took a sip of his soup.

"I did," Vaughn affirmed, his focus still on Milburn. That man would bear watching over the next few days. He was the sort of man who would seek revenge if his plans were foiled—which meant his threatened blackmail might yet come into play. He only hoped Mr. Craig was making some progress on that front.

Vaughn spent the remainder of the meal dividing his attention between his dinner companions. The man on his left, Mr. Chatwin, was the one who had graciously switched places with him.

After dinner, the ladies returned to the drawing room while the men proceeded to the billiard room for port and cigars. Vaughn didn't really wish to play, nor did he wish to smoke and converse with anyone. He was careful to slip out of the room once the others were sufficiently distracted.

A cold voice disrupted his walk down the hall. "I know what you're doing." Vaughn froze next to a marble bust of a noble lady and turned to see Milburn closing the door of the billiard room behind him.

He forced himself to relax, even though every muscle inside him was ready for a fight. "What, pray tell, is that?"

"You and that little fool. She thinks she can outsmart me by bringing you here. But I'm no fool. We both know you really don't want to marry her. So what is she giving you? Sharing her bed wouldn't be enough. It must be something else. Is she paying you? Whoring out for your services? I know you are desperate enough, but I still can't believe you'd be such a *pathetic* man." Milburn *tsked* snidely. "How far the Darlington name has fallen."

Vaughn's hands curled into fists at his sides, but there was no point in bashing the man's head, even if it would feel bloody good. He drew in a slow, calming breath.

"You are mistaken. I am going to marry her, and I'm not desperate. It seems to me *you* are the desperate one. Are you angry she refused you? Maybe you shouldn't have shoved your last mistress out a window. Or maybe it's because you attempted to blackmail her. That tends to dampen any romantic notions a lady might have for a man. Unlike you, I don't hurt women."

"Oh, but you do." Milburn countered, his voice quiet but clear in the hall. "We both know what kind of man you are. Does she know what you need? How you find your pleasure? Someone should warn the poor girl." Milburn's grin was so arrogant Vaughn actually took a step forward, ready to raise his hand against him.

Milburn opened the billiard room door. A couple of heads turned their way, wondering who was about to enter.

"Careful, Darlington. I wouldn't want to see you thrown out of the house for brawling. Then no one would be there to comfort Miss Darby. Oh wait, *I* would. Go ahead, throw a punch."

With a low growl, Vaughn lowered his fist and forced a smile.

"You're hardly deserving of such attention. If you were any more beneath my notice, I'd have to check the bottom of my boot heel to find you." Before he could let Milburn antagonize him further, he went upstairs to his room.

It was going to be a long wait until midnight. He would have to distract himself from thoughts of making Milburn bleed, instead picturing how he would enjoy spending time with Perdita beneath the kissing boughs in the hidden alcove of the library.

CHAPTER 8

Perdita waited for her lady's maid to lay out her nightgown.

"Beth, would you be upset if I called you after midnight to undress me?"

Beth, a sweet girl with reddish-brown hair, glanced at her in surprise.

"Miss?" Beth never asked direct questions, but Perdita knew this was her maid's way of inquiring.

"You remember what I told you about Milburn?" Perdita had confessed her fears a few weeks before.

"I do." Beth took one of Perdita's dresses and smoothed out the wrinkles before carrying it to the tall armoire.

"Well, I am to have a secret rendezvous with Lord Darlington tonight."

"Miss..." Beth's tone was full of reprimand. Her maid could say so much with one word.

"I know you don't approve, but he is the only chance I see of escaping Milburn's interest. We're going to arrange for him to see us somehow. I hope that will dissuade him."

Beth gave a huff of disagreement.

Perdita placed her hands on her hips. "What is it?"

"Miss, there's no reason a man would want a secret rendezvous with you. Not unless he has a specific desire in mind."

"Beth, he doesn't *want* me, not in that way. Men like Darlington are excellent at playing the role of seducer, but that's all it is. Playacting. I paid my price to him by arranging a meeting with Lord Lennox after the New Year. That is all Darlington truly wants."

Her maid gave another disgruntled sound. "You are one of the sweetest and loveliest ladies I know, miss. He'd either be blind or a fool not to want you, and his eyesight seems to be just fine. I'm only asking you to take care. That's all."

"I promise." Perdita knew Vaughn had enjoyed their time in the library and the woods, but she knew men like him. He could have his pick of ladies who knew what to do to please a man, and she could not possibly be interesting enough for him. Vaughn would have no designs upon her, not in the way her maid feared. She was a virgin, and he'd made it abundantly clear upon their first meeting that he didn't seduce "innocents," as he'd called them, yet he had said he might make an exception for her.

"I shall wait up for you," Beth said, clearly unconvinced.

"Go on to bed. If I need you, I'll come and wake you."

Her maid frowned. "You shouldn't have to come fetch me in the servants' quarters, miss."

"Stop worrying." Perdita shoved her out the door. "Go on to bed now."

When her servant was gone, she waited in her room, trying to pass the time until the appointed hour. She tried to read a book, but she couldn't focus. Finally, she left for the library ten minutes before midnight. She was nervous and excited, but it was only because she was engaging in her second midnight rendezvous, *not* because she was excited to see Vaughn again.

When she reached the library, she ducked inside and began to pace, her slippers wearing paths in the carpet by the fire. At the sound of the door opening she turned, an eager smile upon her lips which quickly faded when she saw who it was.

"Finally, we have a moment alone," said Samuel Milburn.

Perdita was afraid to move. Afraid to breathe. All she could think was that he'd once thrown a woman out a window and that she could meet the same dreadful end.

For a long moment, they simply stared at each other, like a cat watching a mouse frozen with fear. Then he walked toward her. Perdita was torn between the desire to run and to hold her ground. This was her house, by God. Who was he to menace her in it? And by the dark look in his eyes she sensed running would only make things worse—and things were already very bad indeed.

Her heart pounded inside her chest, but she tried to remain outwardly calm.

"Darlington will be here in a few minutes. It would be wise of you to leave." She took two slow, careful steps to place a tall armchair between herself and Milburn. The crackling fire and the ticking of the old clock above the marble mantle were strangely loud in the tense silence of the room.

Milburn wore no coat, and made a show of rolling the sleeves of his shirt up. It was intimidating, not that Perdita could explain why. If Vaughn had done the same action, she would not have been afraid but rather excited.

"When I am done with you, he won't care. He certainly won't *want* you any longer." It was her only warning. Milburn lunged for her, and Perdita, too terrified to scream, simply acted. She shoved the chair at him. It wasn't as heavy as it looked and it toppled over, striking him in the knees. He crumpled onto it with a violent shout.

Perdita raised her skirts and ran for the door. But something snatched her ankle, and she fell. When she tried to scramble to her feet, she was pulled back to the ground. Pain shot up her right leg. She kicked out instinctively, again and again.

"Stop that, you little bit—" The hoarse curse turned into a grunt of pain as her foot connected with Milburn's face.

She had only a few precious seconds of freedom, but her palms, slick with sweat, found no purchase on the wooden floor.

"*Help!*" she screamed, but a heavy weight came down on top of her, crushing her into the floor. Air rushed out of her lungs, and a hand dug into her hair, lifted her head up, then shoved it hard on the ground. Her forehead struck the wood floor, dazing her.

"Little bitch. How *dare* you," Milburn growled, his body pinning hers down. His other hand slid toward her skirts, dragging them up.

Perdita's head throbbed in pain, and she couldn't breathe and couldn't move.

The library door was only ten feet away, but it might as well have been ten miles. Her eyes blurred with tears as the horror of what was happening sank in. She dug her nails into the wood, the scraping sound an undertone beneath Milburn's growl as he jerked her skirts higher and panted.

The creak of the library door opening did not stop him, if he had noticed it at all, but Perdita raised her head at the sound, praying someone, *anyone* would see.

"Help—" She tried to shout again, but her lungs were crushed and her vision was tunneling. She couldn't breathe.

There was a distant roar, as though coming deep from a well beneath layers of water, far away. The crushing pressure on her chest vanished, and her ears filled with the harsh, violent sounds of men shouting and furniture crashing.

She crawled toward a bookcase, using the wood to support her as she took shelter, guarding her head as she gasped for breath, her eyes closed. When the sounds stopped and she opened her eyes, she saw Vaughn had hold of Milburn's shirt with one hand and was shaking the unconscious ruddy-faced bastard. When he seemed satisfied the other man was out cold, he dropped him onto the floor, then turned to her. His eyes were hard as diamonds, sharp and burning. His knuckles were covered in blood.

Perdita's lips quivered, and a sob escaped her. His gaze softened, and he rushed over to her, lifting her into his arms.

"My darling, my darling." He buried his face in her hair as he carried her out of the room. He walked hastily down the corridor and back up the stairs. "Which way is your room?" he asked.

"The last one on the left." She tucked her face against his throat, her body still shaking. He carried her to her bedchamber and set her down on her bed, then touched her face, lifting it so he could see her eyes. The anger had returned.

"There is something I must attend to. I will fetch your maid at once."

"No!" she said with a gasp. "I mean, please, do not wake her. She would only worry and ask questions that I'm not ready to answer."

"Are you sure?" Vaughn hesitated at the door. "Will you be all right to be left alone for a few minutes?"

She nodded. She didn't want Beth witnessing her shame and fear. She only wanted Vaughn. He made her feel safe.

"Good. I will return shortly." He placed a kiss upon her brow and left.

Perdita sat there on the edge of the bed and looked down. She was missing one slipper, her gown had been ripped in several places, and her forehead throbbed. She extended her ankle and whimpered at the sharp twist of pain she felt. A minute later, the door opened and her father came in, Vaughn behind him.

"Perdy?" Her father rushed to her side, hugging her. After he was certain she was in no immediate danger, he nodded at Vaughn. "Come. We'll take care of this right now."

She didn't know what they were talking about and was too distraught to ask.

They both left her alone again. When they returned, her mother was with them, and both Vaughn's and her father's boots were covered in fresh snow.

"Papa..." Perdita whispered.

"You're safe now," her father growled. Perdita exhaled, relief sweeping through her, but it didn't erase her humiliation or the pain she was in. Her mother came to her, hugging her fiercely, a stark look of fury and fear in her eyes that filled Perdita with guilt.

But then she remembered Milburn's threats. By tossing him out of the house, Vaughn and her father had given Milburn the excuse he needed to carry out his threats. Her father would soon be exposed for a crime Perdita was certain he was not guilty of. She covered her stomach with her hand as she endured a wave of nausea.

"Perdy, dear, are you all right?" her mother demanded. Then she spun on Vaughn. "What happened to her? What did you do?"

"Mama, please!" Perdita gasped. "He saved me from Milburn."

"What? Milburn? But that's not possible."

"I'm afraid it is," her father said. "Darlington and I just threw the bastard out into the snow."

"That is all?" Her mother's voice rose. "Reginald, you need to go out and find that man and shoot him. Do you understand me?"

"As much as I adore your thirst for vengeance, my dear, we cannot shoot a man in the back. Not even the local magistrate would allow that."

"Then shoot him in the front! The local magistrate be damned!" her mother snarled like a protective wolf.

"Darby, she needs a doctor. Can you send a lad to ride to the village? I'd go, but I will not leave her here alone." Vaughn approached the bed and gingerly cupped her cheek, trying to offer her a reassuring smile, but he faltered.

"Perdita..." For some reason that tenderness, *his* tenderness broke her last bit of strength that had kept up her composure. She burst into tears, slid away from her mother, and reached for him. He curled his arms around her body, delicately at first, before his hold tightened. The warmth of his chest and his dark masculine scent mixed with a hint of winter chill that clung to his clothes soothed her.

She knew her parents were speaking, but she didn't want to face them. Not yet. "Vaughn, make them go to bed, please. I don't want them to stay up and worry. I need to be alone."

He cleared his throat. "I understand, sweetheart." He let go of her and walked over to where her anxious parents stood. Perdita turned away and lay upon her bed, her face buried in the blankets.

"Leave her alone? With you? Absolutely not!" Perdita's mother hissed and came over to her by the bed so that Perdita couldn't avoid her gaze.

"Mama, I wish to be left alone. But I would feel safer if Lord Darlington remained with me."

"But..." Her mother struggled for words. "We have guests. It isn't..."

Perdita sat up and grasped her mother's hands. "I don't care one whit about scandal right now. He saved me from a man who deserves far worse from them. Let them wag their tongues about Milburn's actions, not Vaughn's."

Her mother's lip quivered, and she stared at Perdita for a long moment before she nodded. "Very well. You are engaged, after all..." Then she turned to Vaughn. "If you do anything..." Fury flashed in her mother's eyes.

"I won't." Vaughn's tone was completely serious. Perdita lay back down and closed her eyes, wishing for the humiliation and pain of this moment to end.

She heard the door close. The candles by the bed were snuffed out except for one, which remained close to her side of the bed.

"They are gone. If you decide at any moment that you wish them to return, I will fetch them at once. They will bring the doctor when he arrives, and you will see him for your injuries. I insist upon that." Vaughn's voice was firmer now. The natural command in his tone was a comfort. But she was afraid of his tenderness, afraid it came from a place of pity and not affection.

The tears coating her cheeks dried and made her skin tingle. Affection? She wanted Vaughn's affection? When had that become a concern?

"Perdita?" She flinched when he touched her shoulder. He moved his hand, and she immediately missed him.

She sniffed. "Vaughn, please don't pull away. I'm still rather jumpy after..." She couldn't face the awful horror of what almost happened. He stood beside the bed, his eyes glowing and his hair falling over them. His hands were still bloodied, and she realized his skin was broken in a few places.

She sat up and reached for his hands, catching them before he could pull them away. "You're hurt."

"It's only a scratch or two." He pulled his hands away from hers and walked over to the washbasin, dipping his hands into the water.

"Damn, it's cold," he muttered, and wiped his hands on the spare cloth beside the basin. When he turned to face her again, his grim expression made her stomach clench in anxious knots.

"What happened tonight with Milburn..." He paused, and she knew with dreadful certainty what he was going to say. So she decided to beat him to it.

"I understand. Milburn cannot possibly expect to take my hand now. You've done more than I asked. You are free to return to London. I will have my father announce the breaking of the engagement tomorrow."

He quirked one brow. "That is not what I was going to say." He took a step toward her, then halted as if rethinking his closeness.

"You weren't?" A silly girl's hope flooded through her. The bargain was over, and he had no reason to stay, even though she wanted him to.

"I was going to say that given everything that has happened, I think it's best if we see this through to its end." He looked down at his boots, his voice strangely quiet. "I brought a special license with me."

She wasn't sure what he meant, and her head was aching something fierce. "Vaughn, please, say what you mean." She touched her forehead. The spot where she'd hit the floor was still tender.

"We ought to marry. As soon as possible. Perhaps Christmas Day? That would give you tomorrow, Christmas Eve, to plan a small ceremony at the local church."

Perdita was speechless. Marriage? Was he serious? She had only just admitted to herself that she liked him.

"I know this is sudden and unexpected, but I believe it is a good solution. Milburn won't stop, until you're properly protected as the wife of a peer. Only then will you be safe. I fear, however, that it won't stop him from hurting your father with his supposed evidence, but we shall weather the scandal together. I am no stranger to those." There it was, her safety, his only reason for proposing a hasty marriage. Not because of love or even infatuation, but a simple desire to protect her.

Some ladies would find that chivalrous act enough reason to say yes, but not her. Whenever she had contemplated marriage, it had always been with one thought in mind—to marry for love. A great, all-consuming, passionate love whose flame would challenge even the stars.

"Shall I tell your parents you agree?" he asked.

The silence in the room grew until she felt once again she couldn't breathe.

"No."

He stared at her, his gaze inscrutable, before he began to chuckle wryly.

"You find it amusing that I've rejected you?" She sniffled, tears burning her eyes. She would not cry—*she would not*.

"I think it is, yes. I suppose it's because I mistakenly believed that you bore some *tendre* for me. You don't, do you?"

"I…" She *did* care about him, but that wasn't why she'd refused him. It was because *he* didn't care about her, not in the way she wanted. Her hesitation lit his eyes with a soft fire that left her speechless.

"So, you do care. How curious. What, pray tell, is holding you back then?" He eased down on the bed beside her. He looked so inviting, so charming at that moment, with his hair ruffled and his coat gone. She wanted nothing more than to crawl onto his lap and cover his face with kisses and forget the world outside the room. But she couldn't, he didn't care about her.

"Perdita, we can be honest with each other, can't we?" he asked, cupping her chin gently and turning her face toward his. A tear trailed down her cheek. He caught the bit of moisture delicately with his finger, the way one would catch a dewdrop from a flower's petal.

"You don't...you don't love me. And I understand. This was an arrangement meant to solve both our problems. But you go too far. I could never marry a man unless he loved me. Loved me madly. Loved me to distraction. I deserve a great love. Even you deserve that. We cannot marry simply to afford me protection from Milburn. It is not reason enough."

Vaughn brushed the pad of his thumb over her cheek, his eyes a pair of dark sapphires.

"I do not know if I'm capable of love, but I care for you more than I have for any other woman. And that is no idle boast. When I'm with you, things seem sharper, clearer." He seemed to struggle with his words. "It was as though I was in a listless, hazy dream. When I first kissed you in London, I woke up, clear as a bell ringing in my ears. Everything seems more real, more true when I'm with you." He closed his eyes and shook his head. Then he leaned forward and pressed his forehead to hers, holding her face in his hands.

"I don't know *how* to love, if I am honest. But I don't want to stop this. It was always a charade for you, but it never was for me. I *always* wished to marry you."

She stared at him, pulling her face away from his, but only to see his expression more clearly. "What?"

"Yes. The night you came to my townhouse, I decided then that I wished to marry you."

"But..." How could he have made that decision then? It didn't seem possible.

"Take this chance with me," Vaughn said. "Say you will marry me. We need only the vicar at the church and a gown for you. I even have my wedding clothes ready. They're a tad old, I'm afraid, as I couldn't afford a new set." His face reddened at the confession.

Perdita's heart raced wildly again. Could she do this? Marry him on a leap of faith that he *might* one day love her?

"Answer one question."

"Ask it." He continued to stroke her cheek, the gesture sweet and soothing. How unlike the cold rake she'd believed him to be. Perhaps he could surprise her one day with love. He made her want to believe anything was possible.

She watched him carefully. "*Why* do you care for me? What makes me different from any other young heiress you could marry to satisfy your debts?"

Vaughn didn't pull away, but he didn't respond immediately, either. She searched his eyes for any hint of deception but saw only a flicker of hope. "I have had plenty of chances to marry others. Even a reputation such as mine does not scare away the most determined mothers with marriageable daughters or those looking for a tie to a title. Accepting your offer to participate in a false engagement, however, was never about your fortune. If you recall, my terms were to be introduced to Lennox in order to make my own fortune."

Perdita nodded. She couldn't forget or ignore that truth.

"That would have been enough for me. But I've been intrigued by you since I met you at the garden party in September. You had this cleverness about you, and when I learned that you write astronomy articles, well..."

"You know about that?" Her heart leapt into her throat.

"Of course, I do. The penmanship on the draft you showed me is very feminine, but I suspect you would alter that when you felt it was ready to present. I adore that you write, that you think, that you defy the role society has set for you. Do you have any idea how refreshing that is in a woman? I quite love that about you."

"Would you demand I stop if we married?" she asked quietly, hope and fear warring inside her.

"Stop? Heavens no. I'd encourage it. I've never wanted a normal life, let alone a normal wife. I want a woman who will not shy from trouble, who defies convention, who loves it when I tell her to be good in bed and trusts me to teach her about passion.

You've always been the answer for me, Perdita. Don't you see? I could marry no one else *but* you."

He smiled then, that boyish smile she'd seen in the woods, the one that made her chest tighten and her head feel faint.

"You promise our marriage would be one that would not trap us both? I cannot agree to being trapped in a gilded cage."

"Nor could I. If there's one thing I'm certain of, its that marrying you would be thrilling." He dropped his gaze to her lips, still smiling. "What's it to be?" he asked. "Give this rogue a proper chance? I swear I shall make an excellent husband once I'm reformed, and I quite welcome the challenge."

Perdita sniffed and smiled shyly. "This may be madness, but perhaps for once I should embrace it. I accept." She leaned in the same moment he did, and they kissed. It was a gentle kiss that burned slow and hot, despite the tender brush of lips and the tentative touch of hands upon skin.

When they finally parted, Vaughn carefully touched her forehead with his long, elegant fingers, scowling.

"I wanted to kill that man for what he did to you. I wanted to wring his bloody neck. I was so afraid..."

"I was too, but when I saw you come in the door, I knew you would save me." She crawled into his lap, and he wrapped his arms around her, holding her close.

"I never want you to feel that you need to be saved. But I vow to protect you, to always be there for you, sweetheart." His gently spoken promise made her heart flutter wildly. For the Devil of London to utter such words, it had to be a spell born of magic, the magic of love she hoped for...someday.

At that moment the doctor knocked upon the door. Vaughn reluctantly set her down. She felt his hesitation to let her go. It made her feel warm all over.

"Come in," she called.

Dr. Williams was a middle-aged man with a black bag, and his coat was dusted with snow. Perdita's parents were behind him, both looking anxious.

"Could everyone wait outside, please?" the doctor asked. "You too, lad."

Vaughn didn't leave the bed until she nodded at him. He joined her parents outside, and the doctor set his bag down on the table by the bed.

"There now. Let's take a look at your head first, Miss Darby."

CHAPTER 9

Vaughn wore a path in the Persian rugs covering the floor of the hallway, barely aware that Perdita's parents were watching his every step. On either side of him, paintings of happy lovers seemed to mock him with their innocence.

Mr. Darby fixed him with a formidable gaze. "Darlington, I sense there's more to tonight's events than Milburn suddenly accosting my daughter. I believe you know what's happening, and you had better tell me."

Vaughn took in a deep breath. He stopped pacing. Just beyond her parents, Vaughn could see heavy drapes drawn over the windows to keep out the cold. He stared at them for a long moment, focusing his thoughts before he finally spoke.

"How much do either of you know about Samuel Milburn?"

"Oh, not much," Perdita's mother said, her brows knitting. "He's well set up, and the *ton* seems to approve of him. The society pages paint him as a generous and eligible bachelor. I had no reason to know he was..." She didn't continue, but her eyes blurred with tears.

"I admit I didn't do much asking," said Perdita's father. "I figured if Perdita told me she was interested in him, then I would start asking questions." Darby suddenly paled. "She mentioned... Oh God, she said something about him having a cruel streak, but I didn't listen."

Vaughn crossed his arms over his chest. "Let me tell you what sort of man he is, then. Milburn is a brute and a coward. He killed one of his mistresses, though no one can prove it wasn't an accident. But he bragged about it in the gambling hells. He likes to hurt ladies, force them to his will, break them in ways I will not speak of. That is what he tried to do tonight to your daughter. And he was trying to force your daughter into marriage by threatening you."

"Me?" Mr. Darby looked as if an assassin might pop out at any moment.

"He claims to have documents that prove you have been involved in smuggling goods into the country and he threatened to take that proof to the local magistrate."

Mrs. Darby covered her mouth, her complexion paling. Perdita's father put an arm around her shoulders.

"Breathe, Minerva. Just breathe." He patted her shoulder, keeping a tight hold as he met Vaughn's gaze. "That's utter nonsense. I haven't been involved in any such..." Darby struggled for words.

Vaughn nodded. "I believe you. We think he is working with your investment partners, arranging for you to take the blame for their illegal acts. Perdita feared Milburn and his evidence so much she came to me at my home in London and beseeched me to enter into a false engagement with her. As you may know, I have a somewhat unscrupulous reputation in certain circles. She hoped that an engagement to me would scare Milburn off. Unfortunately, our charade only made the bastard furious enough to attack her. In his twisted mind, he already owned her."

Neither Mr. nor Mrs. Darby spoke for several seconds.

"But... Are you saying you *aren't* going to marry her then?" Mrs. Darby finally asked.

"Far from it. A true affection has grown between us, and she has agreed to proceed with the wedding without false pretenses. Milburn won't dare come after her if I'm there to protect her."

"Why does he want to hurt her? I still don't understand," Mrs. Darby said. "Why didn't he simply blackmail my husband directly? We have plenty of money. He could have demanded we pay him off. Why go after our daughter?"

"Why indeed? That is why I believe the evidence to be false. You would not pay a man off for fabricating a lie."

Mr. Darby nodded at this. "I wouldn't pay him a half penny for such a thing."

"But how could your daughter possibly ask if such a scandalous accusation was true or not? And what if you denied it and she had doubt? That fear is what Milburn preyed on. Sometimes the thought of a misdeed can hold more power than the proof."

Darby shared a knowing look with Vaughn before he continued.

"But it goes beyond that. Do you know the sort of man who buys a spirited horse because he likes to break the beast? He takes pleasure in destroying its spirit and ruining it until it's a mindless, frightened scrap of horseflesh."

Mrs. Darby nodded. Everyone knew that kind of man, a man who would kick a helpless pup or slap a woman for raising her eyes at him. Cruelty was the shield of many cowards.

"He's such a man?" she asked Vaughn. "He saw my daughter's spirit and fire, and he wanted to crush it?"

Vaughn sighed and nodded. "If we can save Perdita from him, then all we need to worry about is Milburn's supposed proof. Even if it is fabricated, he may intend to harm your good name."

Darby clenched his fists. "We can handle that. I'm not so foolish as my partners believe."

"And you, Lord Darlington?" Mrs. Darby asked. "Are you the sort of man to hurt a woman like my daughter?"

"I would sooner end my own life. Perdita's fire and spirit draw me to her. I feel alive in ways I haven't felt in years. It would be an honor to take such a woman as my wife. That is why I offered to marry her. And it's why she accepted. We wish to marry on Christmas Day. I already have the special license and hoped you could both help us arrange the ceremony." A flutter of nerves bubbled up inside him as he waited to see how her parents would react to this.

Mrs. Darby sputtered. "But…that's the day after tomorrow."

"It is, but I see no reason to delay, only to make haste."

Mr. and Mrs. Darby glanced at each other.

"You haven't given us…*reason* to rush this, have you?" Darby asked.

Vaughn shook his head. "My concerns are regarding Milburn only. We've not gone so far in our passions for there to be cause for worry." He admitted this bluntly, smiling a little. "It would seem she draws out the gentleman in me."

"Good. Or I might've tossed you out in the snow as well," Perdita's father replied.

The door to the bedchamber opened. The doctor came out, closing his bag. The silver clasps clicked into place, and he faced them all, his face etched with worry.

"How is she, Henry?" Mr. Darby asked.

"A little shaken up. Her headache was fairly strong. I've given her a bit of a sleeping draught and bound her ankle to keep it from being turned again. She doesn't wish to sleep alone, and she is still anxious. I was told she was attacked?"

"Yes," Darby said. "The gentleman guilty of that act has been cast out of this house."

"Good. She did not say if…" The doctor flushed. "How far the attack went."

Vaughn understood what he wasn't saying. "I stopped him before he could harm her in that fashion."

The doctor's shoulders sagged with relief. "Good. You are Lord Darlington, I take it?" Vaughn nodded. "She wishes to see you again. I asked if she wished to have her maid sent for, but she has declined. She only wants Lord Darlington."

"Thank you." Vaughn walked past him to enter Perdita's bedchamber, but he paused in the doorway, staring at her father.

"I will stay the night with her. On my honor, my intentions are pure."

Darby stared at him and nodded. "Very well." He held his hand out to the doctor. "Let me see you to a room upstairs, unless you wish to ride home."

"Thank you. I think I will stay the night." The doctor followed Perdita's father down the hall. Only Perdita's mother lingered.

"Tell me you will love her," she said earnestly. "After hearing what might have become of my daughter, I need to hear it."

"I've never been in love, madam," he replied solemnly. "But if there was ever someone worthy of my heart, it is she. Although I doubt I'm worthy of hers."

For a moment, he saw Perdita clearly in her mother's face. Had he really thought she was once a silly woman? Now he saw her as her daughter and husband did. A caring mother, a loving wife, a woman who wanted what was best for her child.

"That's not exactly the answer I wished to hear."

"I know," he replied with a soft smile. "But you deserve the truth."

"Do you really believe I'll let you go in there with my daughter and spend the night after admitting you do not love her?" the lady challenged.

Vaughn paused with his hand on the door latch. "I admit to not feeling love; that does not mean I feel nothing. I am fond of her, so much so that I would pledge myself to her protection even if her heart belonged to another. She is frightened and ashamed of what happened to her, afraid that Milburn will come for her. I've seen women in her condition. They jump at every shadow. Even if you stayed with her and locked the door, she would not feel truly safe. I, on the other hand, will sit in a chair with a pistol aimed at the door all night if that is what is required."

Mrs. Darby studied him hard, but at last she relented. "Very well. But if you hurt her..."

"Yes, I know. Your husband has mentioned my being buried where none shall find me on more than one occasion." Vaughn offered her a wry smile before he slipped into the room and closed the door behind him.

He wished he could have said he loved Perdita, but he still didn't know what being in love was like. He'd loved his brother, Edward. The love for a brother was a fierce love, a love that had rough edges and a toughness about it. Love for a woman was…well, it had to be different. He sensed that truth in his bones. It wasn't lust, and it wasn't friendship. What was it?

I want to love her. I want so badly what Gareth and Ambrose have found with their wives.

But the truth was he was afraid his heart was so hardened by his life that it could never soften enough to open up for another soul.

He studied her room before he faced her. He had been far too focused on her to notice anything before.

A telescope stood close to a set of French windows that opened onto a balcony. His little secret scientist and her tools. Half a dozen pillows were on the bed or chairs, and when he studied one more closely, he noticed the needlework showed familiar shapes. Constellations. The stich work wasn't flawless by any means, and he suspected that she spent her time better by penning essays than practicing with a needle and thread. Rather than a dainty escritoire, she had a large desk covered in charts and writings.

Perdita lay on the bed, her eyes half-open, still glassy from the sleeping draught the doctor had given her. Around her, the bed hangings of a soft rose silk brocade with leafy patterns made her look like a princess half-asleep in her bed.

"Vaughn, you will stay, won't you? I'm afraid of even the shadows."

He came over to the bed and brushed the hair back from her cheek. "I'm going to stay. We should get you changed. Can you sit up?"

She struggled to sit up, and he knelt at her feet and removed her remaining slipper. Then he slid his hands up her skirts, removing her stockings. She placed her hands on his shoulders to keep her balance when she stood. He stroked her legs gently, and then he had her turn to face the bedpost. She did so without question while he unfastened the buttons down the back of her gown. And then it fell to the floor. Then she tugged her petticoats down, revealing a perfect set of hips and rounded behind.

"Almost done," he promised, eyeing her stays. He took care to unlace them gently and not tug too hard so she didn't lose her breath. Then they too fell to the ground. She stepped out of them, wearing only the loose chemise that came down to her knees. Vaughn pulled back the bedclothes and urged her to get under the covers. She sighed and curled up against her pillow, her hair falling in loose tumbles over it. He plucked the pins out of her hair one by one, then gently massaged her scalp to make sure there were no pins left.

Perdita sighed. "For the Devil of London, you have turned out to be quite an angel."

"Am I?" he asked. The Devil of London. That nickname had always amused him. Given his choice of bed play, added to his reputation at the gambling tables, the *ton* had awarded him the unfortunate moniker.

"Yes." She reached behind her to catch his arm and pulled him into the bed. "Lie with me."

It was a command. Her eyes locked with his, and even though her gaze was soft and a little distant from the draught she'd taken, he saw the glint of determination to get her way.

He wasn't about to ignore it. He removed his boots and slipped in the bed behind her. He curled one arm around her waist, tucking her against him.

"Don't I scare you? You should be afraid of all men after what happened." He wasn't sure why he asked it, knowing the answer could be crushing.

She was quiet, her breathing slow. She wasn't afraid of him.

"Not all men are the same. And not all men saved me. Milburn is a monster. You...? You are my white knight."

"I am no white knight, as much as I wish I could be. I'm afraid my armor is tarnished rather than shining."

Perdita stroked his cheek with delicate fingertips, her eyes grave. "A knight in shining armor is a man whose metal has never been tested. And you have proven more than once just how strong your *mettle* is."

Her words made his heart clench tight and she didn't miss his play on metal and mettle. How could she know just the thing to say that made him feel both cut open and exposed, yet unafraid? Vaughn closed his eyes and sighed before he spoke again. "What can I do? Tell me and I will do *anything* for you."

"Are you sure? You might not like what I ask."

Vaughn expected some vow of vengeance against Milburn—which he would be happy to oblige. "Anything."

"Then I wish to *know* you."

That caught Vaughn short, and he wasn't sure he was prepared for it. "Know me?"

"If we are to be married, I wish to know everything about you. I wish to know the man, not just the persona he woos women with." She rolled over in his arms, and he could see her face, accented by winter moonlight.

His heart pounded. Would she even *like* such a man? One who was simply a person to her and not doing and saying the things he knew she wanted to hear? "What do you want to know about me?"

"Tell me something wonderful. Something that you cling to when the shadows threaten to drown you." She put one hand to his jaw, her fingers exploring along his skin. Her touch burned in a wonderful way that made his heart skip.

"Something wonderful..." He would say this moment, but she was searching for his past. Something that revealed the true Vaughn to her. He swallowed thickly, knowing the memory he would share with her.

"I had a brother, Edward, who was older than me by five years."

"I didn't know you had a brother." Her eyes, dark in the room, seemed to channel the thin glow of the moonlight from the window, like two pools frosted with ice, yet her gaze wasn't cold. It made him feel warm to have such intensity focused on him.

"Edward was...well, perfect, and I mean that in the best way. He was intelligent, amusing, generous—he was simply the *best*. Our parents were drawn to him, as the eldest and the favored. But I didn't hate him or the long shadow his life cast over mine. Far from it—he made me happy to be me, just Vaughn, Edward's little brother. We would go riding in the late summer, just the two of us, racing through the glens. He *always* let me win. Even when my gelding threw a shoe once, he stopped his horse, walked back to me, and announced I had beaten him. That was exactly the sort of man he was. And I could never measure up to that." His voice caught on the last few words, and he didn't speak for a moment.

Perdita's fingers stilled on his throat, and he felt her tremble. "What happened to him?"

Vaughn tried to smile. "Let's leave it at that. You asked for something wonderful, after all."

"I asked to know everything about you. Good and bad. What happened?"

Vaughn's throat felt like he had swallowed shards of glass. "He went riding alone one day. I was only sixteen at the time. I was away at Eton, and he was tending to the estate. He was thrown from his horse and died from the fall."

He shut his eyes, holding Perdita close, clinging to her as pain that he'd buried long ago clawed its way up. He remembered receiving the letter at his rooms in Eton. His mother's spidery handwriting on the parchment was blotted with tears as she'd informed him Edward had died. His heart, whatever had still been open to life and love, had turned to stone that day.

"You loved him dearly," she said.

"I did." He dared not open his eyes, because the treacherous tears would cling to his lashes.

"That means you *can* love, Vaughn. It means that someday you might even love *me*." She brushed one finger over his lips, as though memorizing the shape and the feel of them.

A strange tremor ran through Vaughn. He thought back on each kiss he'd stolen from her, how she'd returned that fire, but it had always seemed like something *more* in a way he couldn't describe. To hear her speak of love, of hoping that someday he would love her, he realized then that she was telling him that *she* loved him. It was frightening and exciting, and he didn't know what to do except hold on to her and breathe as emotions ran riotously through him.

In that moment, he knew that if he lost Perdita, he would never recover, never come back from such devastation.

"Sleep now. I am here to watch over you." He kissed her brow, and she tucked herself tighter against him. All would be well. He had to believe that.

CHAPTER 10

Perdita did not wake until midday. The bed was empty, but the imprint where Vaughn had lain was still warm to the touch. She had been so tired after taking the sleeping draught, but she hadn't forgotten what he'd told her about his brother, about loving and losing him. She had seen the pain in his eyes and heard the catch in his voice. Her viscount's heart was not made of stone or even ice. It was there, beating and bleeding, just like her own.

She climbed out of bed, wincing at the stiffness of her muscles. It was going be a long day, and tonight was the supper and the ball, which meant she'd have little time for rest. She lifted her head when her maid came in.

Beth came over and gave her a gentle hug. "My lady. I was told about last night by your mother. I am so sorry! Why didn't you send for me?"

"It's all right, Beth." She patted Beth's back before she released her. "I didn't wish to wake you, and honestly...I wanted to be left alone after what happened." She wouldn't admit to Beth that she'd been ashamed of being attacked and that she'd felt foolish.

Her maid stared at her before she spoke, as though she understood Perdita's feelings. "I do wish you had sent for me. I wouldn't have..." Beth struggled for words. "You're *my* lady, and I would have done anything to help you." The maid hugged her again. Perdita's eyes pricked with tears as she patted the girl's back.

"Thank you, Beth." For a long moment, neither of them spoke, but when Beth straightened, Perdita had banished her fear and was acting as normal as possible.

"I've been given strict orders that you are to remain off your feet, miss, except for dinner. And you are not allowed under *any* circumstances to dance."

"But—"

"Not one step." Beth began to lay out a fresh dress and slippers. It was a white gown.

"Please, not that one. Surely I can at least choose what I wear."

Beth gave her a challenging stare. "And just *which* gown did you expect to wear?"

"I was hoping to wear my blue gown, the one with the white roses on the bodice and sleeves. I wish to wear a new gown, and it will help me stand out among the other ladies who will likely wear white, red, or green to celebrate Christmas Eve."

"Very well, the blue one. But no dancing," Beth commanded.

Perdita rolled her eyes and let her maid help her get dressed. She discovered a small purple bruise on her face that she would to try to hide with her hair. It would be difficult, though. She hoped no one would notice.

An hour later, she was walking to the kitchens, hoping to steal a few biscuits. She'd had no appetite early this morning, but now she was feeling more like herself at last and was a bit peckish. She was shocked to see Vaughn join her at the stairs leading down to the kitchen.

"How are you?" he asked. He put one hand on the small of her back. Despite the layers of fabric between them, she could feel the heat of his palm through it all.

She ducked her head, embarrassed to face him with the bruise so visible on her face. "Well enough."

Vaughn stopped at the bottom of the stairs and cupped her chin, lifting her face up to face his.

"Damn," he cursed softly. "It looked less dark earlier this morning before I left."

This morning. So he had left just before she'd woken and kept his promise to stay the night with her.

"It is fine. I'm just afraid to let any of the guests see. Scandal and gossip travel so fast."

"That it does." He touched her hips with his hands, the hold gentle but firm. "Why don't we meet in the library in one hour? I have a plan."

"I was going to fetch something to eat."

"I will take care of it. Now go rest and meet me in the alcove. One hour."

"All right." She lifted her skirts to go back upstairs, but he captured her arm, halting her so that he could steal a deep kiss, and then he released her. Breathless, she stood there for a moment, her body hot enough that she wanted to run out into the snow to cool herself. Then he headed down the corridor to the kitchens, and she went back up to her chamber, wondering what he had planned.

She had her answer an hour later when she tiptoed into the library. She gasped.

Vaughn stood on the edge of the window seat, seeing to the hanging of a large kissing bough. At his feet on the floor was a large blanket with plates of food and a pitcher of lemonade with two glasses. Several books were in a neat stack by the blankets and pillows arranged against the wall. He'd created a picnic for just the two of them.

What man would take such time and effort to produce a lovely little scene such as this? It was utterly charming. She sniffed as her eyes burned. The blow to her head made her feel quite silly. It did not escape her notice that he had taken a room she loved, a room where something terrible had happened, and made it feel like a safe place again. And to think he believed he wasn't a gentleman...

He still had his back to her, and she admired the lean lines of his legs and the firmness of his backside in his dark-blue trousers. He was not wearing knee britches, but he would change later when he went to the ball...without her. She was going to miss dancing with him, miss dancing in general until her ankle healed and the doctor thought she could chance a quadrille or two.

"You've outdone yourself," she said as she reached the picnic blanket.

Vaughn flashed a brilliant smile as he climbed down from the window seat. They both stood beneath the kissing bough now. Outside the snow glittered on the lawns, painting a pretty winter picture that made her heart leap.

He nodded at the bit of greenery that would no doubt lead to something very wicked. "Care to put it to use?"

"I think that's a wonderful idea." She stood up on tiptoe to curl her arms around his neck. At the same moment he lifted her up by the waist and kissed her. His lips were soft yet gentle as he explored her mouth. Perdita gave in to the exquisite taste of him and the heat of his body. He made her forget her worries. Surely that made him perfect.

When their lips parted, he stared at her in wonder.

"What is it?"

"You." He brushed the backs of his knuckles over her cheek. "Even after what Milburn tried to do to you, you can stand here and kiss me. You're astonishing."

A flutter of panic rose in her at his words. Did he think her wanton or unaffected by last night?

"Whatever you are thinking, stop," he said. "What I meant is that few women would be as brave as you to even be alone with a man after what happened."

She lowered her gaze to the floor. "What happened to me... That doesn't make me weak. It doesn't make me less."

"Yes," he agreed. "You are strong. You always have been."

She raised her gaze to his, hoping she would see no condemnation in his eyes.

"And that strength makes you astonishing." He feathered his lips over hers in a light, sweet, tender kiss that made her knees weak. For a man who claimed he could not love, he could kiss like one who loved more than the most romantic of poets.

"Would you like to sit down? We may have our picnic, even if it is a little bit late." Vaughn helped her down on the blanket and began to serve the cold cuts and the fruit he'd brought up from the kitchen.

"Vaughn, when we are married, are we to move into your town-house?" she asked. It was strange to think she was to be married so soon, to the Devil of London, no less. It was equally strange to think that the *ton* had favored Milburn as a gentleman and condemned Vaughn in the same breath, yet society couldn't have been more wrong about both men.

At least my devil is really an angel in disguise.

"We could, unless you wish to move to a different residence." He answered carefully, his words measured. "I've had to close up the country estate." He didn't say it, but she knew what he wasn't saying. That he wouldn't use her money to reopen the estate unless she allowed him to use her money for such a purpose.

She took a drink of her lemonade and looked at him.

"Last night when you spoke of Edward, I sensed you were unhappy. I want you—*us*—to be happy. What if we used some of my dowry to open up your country home? If we are able to fill your tenant farms again, we could have some success at creating a sustainable estate. I admit, I prefer the country to London and would enjoy living in the house where you grew up, if you wish." For them and the children she hoped would come. She had never been interested in children before, but when she looked at Vaughn and pictured children with his golden hair and blue eyes...she wanted them desperately.

"If you don't mind, I would like that. But I assure you, once my investments with Lennox bear fruit, I will restore the money we used to your accounts. People will talk, of course, when we move to the estate. They'll say my marrying you was only to improve my family's name and my circumstances." Heavy regret layered his tone, and it softened her heart even further.

"Let them talk." She met his gaze. "It is nothing we haven't heard said of a hundred others. You and I know the truth of what lies between us."

She pushed her plate off the blanket and held out a hand to him. The afternoon sun from the window bathed them both as they sat next to each other on the floor by the window seat.

Vaughn placed his hand in hers, and she pulled gently on his arm. He raised his brows in a silent question. She grinned. There was one thing she wanted more than anything right now. Him. She knew he would have to be tempted after everything that had happened, and she would do whatever she must to convince her gentlemanly rogue to claim what was his. She wanted to erase the bad memories here and cover them with new ones. But more than that, she wanted to be with Vaughn. Not because she wanted to get over Milburn's attack, but because she'd wanted Vaughn before, before all this had happened.

I will not let Milburn take my happiness or my passions from me. I can love and make love without his specter haunting me.

"Tomorrow we are to be married. You have been the perfect gentleman, but I don't want a gentleman right now. I want you, my dangerous rogue, to do what you do best. *Seduce me.*"

His blue eyes darkened, and he crawled over to her as she lay back on the blanket.

"Are you sure? After..." He hesitated, afraid to say the word.

"What Milburn tried to do will not define me, and it hasn't changed how I feel about you."

His lips twitched in a wicked fashion. "Anyone could come in and see us," he warned as he leaned over her prone body.

"They could. But everyone is busy preparing for the dance tonight. Since I'm not allowed to dance, I would much rather be here with you right now, like this."

His wolfish grin made her heart skip. "A wicked lady for a wicked lord—I do believe we are *perfectly* matched." He unbuttoned his waistcoat as she helped him remove his shirt. She flattened her palms over the smooth, sculpted planes of his chest and the corded muscle of his stomach. She clenched her thighs together as a wave of heat rolled through her lower body.

"I WANT TO STRIP YOU OUT OF THAT GOWN, BUT WE CANNOT

risk it." He lowered himself on top of her. She tucked her skirts up, and he settled between her parted thighs. He stroked one hand down her right leg, playing with the ribbons of her garter. Then he slid his hand between their bodies, touching her between her thighs. She jolted at the press of his fingers. She was so aroused, so ready for more, that she tensed against the slight intrusion.

"It will hurt a little," he warned. His eyes blazed with a fire that echoed her own body, and she nodded.

"I know, but I want you." She lifted her hips in encouragement, and he began to kiss her lips and her throat before she felt him fumble with his trousers and shift above her. Something hot and hard nudged at her entrance. She tightened her legs on his hips, trying to draw him closer.

"I am ready," she whispered against his mouth.

Vaughn thrust. In one blinding moment of pain, she welcomed him into her body, and he stilled above her, his breathing hard.

"That's it, darling. Breathe with me." He kissed her gently as he began to rock inside her.

The pain blurred into something different, something sharp, yet not painful. It was a building pleasure. He moved his hips, pulling in and out of her more quickly. The sensation was almost too much to bear. Her breasts ached as they pushed tightly against her bodice.

"Vaughn, it's happening again." Her body burned all over like it was kissed with fire. His lips captured hers, his arms braced on either side of her shoulders. He rose above her, all muscle and power. Yet there was no fear, only pleasure as it ripped through her. She cried out against him and he joined her, harshly cursing as they both went limp.

Every muscle that ached from last night's ordeal was now relaxed. She couldn't have imagined that making love would be so calming once it was done.

"How do you feel, darling?" Vaughn asked, his blue eyes touching upon her face as he searched her gaze.

She sighed and lifted her head, kissing him. "Wonderful."

"Just imagine how much better it will be on a bed, when I can take hours exploring you, my mouth and hands touching secret places on your body."

"Hours?" Lord, she couldn't fathom that.

"*Hours*," he repeated in a low whisper. "And it will make you so exhausted you won't be able to leave our bed."

Our bed. Those two simple words wrapped her heart in a cocoon of warmth.

"We could stay here," she whispered. "Forget dinner and the ball. Let's stay right here." She ran her hands up his arms, relishing the way his muscles felt beneath her fingers. The sunlight created a wild halo of gold as it hit his hair, and she ran her fingers through the burnished strands. The ruby stone of her ring gleamed a dark blood red, like a pulsing heart.

"Is that what you desire, to hide away? Not that you need any excuse after what you've endured. We've plenty of books, but we shall need more food. I'll get dressed and go down to the kitchens, shall I?"

"Yes, please."

He pulled away from her, and they both straightened their clothes. She helped him button his waistcoat, and then he left her alone. She settled into a window seat, her body languid. She could stay here just like this for an age, watching the sun glint off the snow in the gardens. Fresh snow. They'd had more early this morning.

She studied the snow, then leaned carefully against the glass to get a better look. There were footprints...leading right up to the windows of the house one floor below. None of the servants would be outside, not so close to the house. But who would be prowling about in the snow, peering into windows? Only one name came to mind.

Milburn.

He was still here. She would have to tell Vaughn.

CHAPTER 11

Perdita stared at the steps leading down to the coach that would carry her to the small church in Lothbrook. She couldn't ignore the flutter in her belly. In a few hours she would be wife to the Devil of London.

"I cannot believe you are getting married!" Her best friend, Alexandra Worthing, stood next to her, a puzzled look on her beautiful face. "Nor can I believe *who* you are marrying."

Once the rest of society heard the news, she knew she would be flooded with letters from all of her friends and acquaintances, desperate to hear how such a match came about. It would be exhausting to tell everyone.

For a brief moment, she considered reaching out to Lady Society, the infamous mystery woman who penned gossip columns in the *Quizzing Glass Gazette*. That might be a way to tell London the story in a way that would allow Perdita to enjoy her honeymoon without an endless deluge of inquiries.

"I know. But it feels right," Perdita answered. She shifted her bouquet and finally addressed the unspoken tension between her and her friend. "Are you angry with me? For marrying Darlington?

I know after what he did, kidnapping you, that you must despise him..."

Perdita swallowed whatever else she had planned to say. In some ways, Alexandra probably viewed Vaughn the way Perdita viewed Milburn, though Vaughn had never planned on forcing himself on Alex. It had all been for show to win a wager. But she felt she was betraying Alex somehow by marrying him, and the thought was breaking her heart.

"I..." Alex glanced down at her boots. "I am surprised, I admit. I didn't think he would be good enough for you. I'm still not convinced he is, but if you love him and he loves you..."

"He does," Perdita said, though she wasn't sure it was true, at least not yet.

"Then that is all that really matters, not what I think of him." Alex tightened her cloak and held out her hands to Perdita in a way they'd always done as girls. It was a sign of friendship, a sign of trust. Perdita grasped her hands, the bouquet caught between them as they stared at each other.

"It is your wedding day," Alex said with a broad smile. "And our husbands are good friends. Today is a happy day."

"It is," Perdita agreed. "Darlington and I are so happy you came."

"Of course! I had a letter from your mother the moment you told her of your engagement. I'm only sorry we weren't here sooner. Worthing would have helped Darlington drag that bastard out into the snow and drawn his cork!"

"Alex!" Perdita tried not to laugh at her friend's bloodthirsty words.

Alex pointed one booted foot in a ladylike way. "He deserves far worse," she grumbled.

"Yes, he does." For the tenth time that day, she glanced around but saw only her footmen and the coach. It didn't take away the sense she was being watched. She'd told Vaughn yesterday of her fears that Milburn hadn't returned to London. He had vowed to keep a vigil on her at all times, and it was only with her insistence that he even agreed to leave her to go to the church first.

"Come on, Perdy, we mustn't delay." Alex took her arm, and they walked down to the coach and climbed in. Her father came out of the house and joined them, grinning.

"Nothing like a Christmas wedding, eh?" he asked.

Perdita smiled back. What a wonderful day to be married.

VAUGHN FELT THE WEIGHT OF HIS PISTOL TUCKED SECURELY into a pocket of his cloak as he walked up the steps of the small gray stone church. Greenery hung over the doorway and covered many of the pews that lined the aisle leading to the altar. Many of the villagers of Lothbrook were waiting in the pews, wearing their finest Christmas clothing. Everyone had come, it seemed, to witness the wedding.

My wedding. He smiled a little as he removed his cloak, careful to keep the pistol secure as he handed it to his valet, who took it to the front row near the altar and set it down. It was his only protection in case Milburn decided to show up. After Perdita confessed she'd seen footprints outside of the house alongside the windows, he feared Milburn was still somewhere in the village waiting for them.

He'd tried to calm her concerns, but the truth was Perdita was more correct in her fears than she knew.

His butler, Mr. Craig, had arrived the day before with news. Mr. Craig had used his cunning and his contacts from days before to track down Darby's investment partners. After making some inquiries down by the docks, he ransacked their offices during the night and found a couple of hidden ledgers, dating back to several years prior to Darby's involvement. No doubt whatever falsified documents Milburn possessed had used these as their template, with the dates changed accordingly.

Craig had taken the documents to the local magistrate, and the investment partners involved had been taken into custody for further review. Milburn no longer held any power over Perdita, fabricated or not, and the scandal that had broken over London would inevitably ensnare the vile man and ruin his reputation as well. Milburn would be out for blood.

"Stop fidgeting," Ambrose muttered in his ear. "Don't want the bride-to-be to notice you're afraid."

Vaughn swallowed a laugh. When his best friend, Ambrose, had arrived with his new wife, it had been a blessing that Vaughn had never expected. He had almost destroyed their friendship by kidnapping Alex to win a wager. For his friend to be here today, on his wedding day... A thousand words were on the tip of Vaughn's tongue, but he was too ashamed to speak any of them.

"All will be well," Ambrose said, as though he could read the pain and regret in Vaughn's heart.

"Thank you," he whispered. Ambrose nodded, smiling.

The vicar, in his Christmas vestments, waited beside Vaughn. They both stared at the door, listening for the rattle of a coach on the cobblestones, the one carrying his bride-to-be.

"Worried she'll run?" The vicar, a man in his early twenties, chuckled. "Don't be. I've known Miss Darby since I was a lad. There's nothing that will stop her when she wants something. And from what I hear, she wants *you*." The man's eyes twinkled, and Vaughn relaxed.

She did indeed want him, just as he wanted her. The previous evening, he and Perdita had spent hours in the library, reading to each other and making love. It was worth the risk of being discovered to show her how proficient he could be. And she had been perfect. *Wonderfully perfect.*

And now he would join his life to hers before God. For the first time, he understood the strange condition his friend Ambrose had fallen prey to.

Love—love brought on by sheer joy. He never would've imagined he would feel this way. Not after the heartbreak of his brother's death.

The doors opened, and Perdita came into the church wearing a white silk gown. It was simple but elegant, just as she was. She bit her lip as she walked toward him, and he realized she was trying to hide a smile. Mr. Darby led her to him and kissed her cheek before he took his place in the front pew.

The vicar began the ceremony, and Vaughn struggled to hear the words of the vows and sacraments. All he could think about was how he'd bared his soul to this woman beside him and how she had worked her way into his heart with her cleverness and sweetness. His life was now divided into life before her and life with her.

At last he was given permission to kiss her, something he did without hesitation. She giggled against his lips, and they moved to the vestry to sign the register. Then he took his cloak from his valet and she took hers from her maid, and they prepared to meet their guests on the steps of the church.

Mr. Craig stood close by, his cool eyes and weathered face taking in the quaint scene of the Christmas town. Vaughn nodded at him. The older man appeared haughty and aloof to most, but to Vaughn he was a trusted ally, and he was glad Mr. Craig had been able to attend the wedding.

"Are you ready to go?" Perdita asked, eyes bright with mischief.

"I am. Quite ready, that is, to get you flat on your back on a bed." He whispered this so that none of the guests around them could hear.

"Wicked man!" she chastised, but her cheeks had already flushed. He couldn't help but notice how her breasts pressed against the bodice of her gown as she inhaled. Soon he would be exploring every bit of her body with intimate pleasure.

Vaughn was so lost in thoughts of his honeymoon and the coming feast he was distracted as they left the little church. People gathered around them, shaking hands and congratulating. It wasn't until the crowd thinned Vaughn realized something terrible was unfolding.

Samuel Milburn stood in the cobblestone street, disheveled and wild. He stared at them on the steps.

"You've ruined everything!" Milburn shouted and raised his arm. Light glinted off the pistol as he took aim at Perdita.

Vaughn never understood what his father had meant when he'd spoken of a soldier's instincts until that moment. He acted without thought and stepped in front of his wife. The pistol fired, and Vaughn grunted as the bullet struck.

Pain, sharp at first, then dulling to a heavy ache, but he found himself unable to even utter a curse. Around him everyone was screaming, yet Vaughn kept Perdita pressed safely behind him, even as he stumbled and fell. He struggled to pull his weapon from his cloak as Milburn produced a second pistol.

Mr. Craig stepped forward, pressing Vaughn behind him. "Pardon me, my lord," he growled and raised his own pistol, firing at Milburn.

The man fell to his knees and landed facedown in the snow, a red pool of blood seeping into the snow around him on either side, his weapon cocked and still gripped in his hand. For a second no one moved. Then Mr. Craig tucked his empty pistol into his coat and turned back to Vaughn.

"Terribly sorry, sir. But your wound would have hampered your aim."

"Good man." Vaughn chuckled and then winced. "Good man." He'd always been glad his butler had a very particular set of skills, and today those skills had saved him and his wife.

His butler nodded solemnly.

Perdita fell to her knees next to him. "Vaughn."

"I'm all right, darling. Would you mind fetching the doctor?" He kept his voice calm because she was crying and clinging to him. The chaos outside the church had calmed only a little, but he didn't focus on any of that. He kept his gaze on Perdita and hers was on him.

"And to think you were worried I didn't love you," he teased.

Her eyes filled with tears. "Vaughn." She clutched him fiercely. "Please don't joke about that."

He managed to wrap one arm around her as he righted himself.

Only then did he dare to look at his wound. It wasn't deep. He'd been hit in the shoulder, the bullet passing through muscle alone. It was really more of a graze.

"Is it bad?" Perdita asked, holding herself close to him.

"No, not at all. Lucky for us, I'm damned hard to kill."

Perdita stared at him, blinking rapidly as tears formed in her eyes, and Vaughn knew she was upset at his teasing.

The doctor arrived a few minutes later. His residence, thankfully, was not far from the church. Vaughn and Perdita went back inside while his wound was tended. They sat in the last pew, where Vaughn removed his cloak, waistcoat, and shirt.

"Damn, it's bloody cold in here," Vaughn muttered as the doctor cleaned his wound.

"Lucky, that's what you are," Dr. Williams said. "Mostly a graze. I'll bind it up, and you must take care to keep the bandage fresh. No vigorous activity for a few days, I'm afraid." The doctor shot Vaughn a pointed look and then said to Perdita, "I understand young love and the passion of newlyweds, but none of that, you hear? Not for three or four days."

"Like hell," Vaughn growled.

Perdita squeezed his arm. "If he says we mustn't, then we won't. But I shall make up for it. Once we can." Her cheeks pinked in a delightful blush.

"I'll hold you to that promise, darling." He had a few delicious ideas of what he'd do once he was mended.

She smiled back, her eyes sparkling with tears. "Good."

Dr. Williams grunted as he bandaged Vaughn's wound. By the time they were ready to leave the church, they found Perdita's father waiting outside. Milburn's body had been removed from the street.

"Your butler has called for the magistrate, Vaughn. I doubt there will be any further questions. Everyone saw what happened."

"Thank heavens." Perdita rested her head against Vaughn's shoulder. The gesture made his stomach flutter with a quiet sort of thrill, one that lingered and made him feel dizzy.

Mrs. Darby smiled warmly at him. "Let's get you both home."

Home. Home with Perdita and her family. *They are my family now.* With a little grin, he walked with his bride down to the waiting coach, ignoring the twinge of pain in his shoulder. He was not alone. Not anymore.

THREE LONG DAYS LATER, PERDITA FOUND HERSELF SITTING ON the edge of her bed, holding a small box, wearing nothing but her shift. Nerves danced in her chest and belly. She couldn't help it. Tonight she was going to give Vaughn his Christmas gift, albeit a few days late, and she prayed he would not be upset with her.

Many men would not react well to having matters of pride exposed. But in the last few days so much had changed between them. Since they could not make love, they had lain in each other's arms and whispered in the dark about their hopes, their dreams, and their lives before.

It astonished her to realize it was indeed possible to love a man who'd been a stranger to her so recently. Yes, lust had been there, but after everything they'd shared, love had crept up on her, silent as a thief, and now she truly loved him. She knew he loved her too. If stepping between her and Milburn's pistol hadn't been enough, the last three days had proven it. The gentle smiles, the way he listened, the way they'd lain together, their heads close and limbs entwined. Hearts beating as one.

She sat up straighter when her bedchamber door opened.

Vaughn walked in, flashing her a wicked grin that made her laugh.

"Three days, as ordered. And now you're mine. *All mine.*" He started toward the bed, but she held up a hand.

"Wait."

He stopped, his eyes questioning hers. She looked at the little box and thought of what it contained.

Please understand why I must give it back to you.

"What is that?" he asked.

"A Christmas present, long overdue." She raised it up, and he slowly took it from her. He was so beautiful, the way only a man could be while wearing nothing save his buckskin breeches and a dark-blue silk vest. Vaughn opened the box, his eyes locked on the gift.

It was, of course, the pocket watch she'd bought back from the jeweler.

"I..." His voice broke as he took the watch from the box. The silver glinted in the light. "How..." He gave his head a little shake. "This was my grandfather's. I had to sell it."

"You promise not to be angry with me?" she asked.

"I promise." His eyes blazed, though not with anger.

"I saw you, that day at the jeweler's. I didn't mean to see what I did. But once I realized you might be buying me a ring, I couldn't let you give up something I could tell was dear to you."

"All this time you've kept it?"

"I was afraid you would be angry with me for buying it back, but I couldn't leave it there. It belongs to you. You're not upset, are you?"

His thumb brushed over the silver lid of the watch before he set it on the table by her washbasin. He unbuttoned his waistcoat methodically, then removed his shirt. He loosened the placket of his trousers, but didn't remove them.

"Vaughn..."

"Remove your shift," he commanded. His voice was low and dark. His eyes, however, promised that wicked, forbidden fantasies would be fulfilled. She stood uneasily in the wake of his intense gaze. "*Now.*"

She rushed to remove her shift. He plucked it from her hands the moment it was free of her. He folded it and set it on the armchair by her vanity table.

"When we sleep, you will remove your shift. I like to be beside you skin to skin," he murmured as he reached up to trail a finger along her collarbone.

Perdita shivered and moved to cover her breasts, but his dark gaze stopped her.

"In this room, I am in control," he reminded her. She nodded, her body heating. She would never let him control her outside of bed, but in bed she would willingly succumb. She craved his commands, his control. It was both thrilling and exciting.

"Lie back for me, darling."

She did so, trying to lift her head to see him as he retrieved his neckcloth from his shirt.

"What—"

He hushed her as he came back to the bed. He took her wrists and bound them together with the cloth. Then he raised her hands above her head and tied them to one of the bedposts.

Perdita's heart raced. She struggled against the restraints but couldn't get free.

"Here, alone, we can indulge our dark sides," he said, a smile curving his lips at the corners. "Do you trust me?"

"Yes." She did trust him. The bandage around his shoulder reminded her that this man would give his life for her.

"Good." He climbed onto the bed, caging her body as he kissed her. His lips moved expertly over hers. Then he traced a burning path down to her bare breasts. Perdita sucked in air as his lips fastened around one nipple. It was an overpowering sensation to feel his hot mouth on her breasts, sucking. He nipped the tender bud, a whisper of pain blending in with the pleasure before he moved to her other breast. He moved lower and lower down her body. Her thighs clenched together, but he shoved them apart.

"You're such a pretty pink," he whispered against her mound before he kissed her inner thighs. She opened her mouth to speak, but he silenced her with another of his wicked looks.

"You're mine, sweeting. To play with, to taste. You may only say 'my lord' or make sounds of pleasure. Understand?"

She gave a jerky nod and then gasped in shock as he licked her down there. The unexpected burst of sensations had her whimpering, her thighs shaking. His tongue continued playing with her folds and caressing her before he closed his lips around her throbbing bud. Then he sucked on that bundle of nerves, and she screamed in shock at the hard rush of pleasure that exploded through her.

"That's it," he coaxed gently as she drifted down from the exquisite high.

"My lord..." She panted softly, barely able to think past those two words.

"Yes?"

She had closed her eyes, but she could hear the smile in his voice. "You are the most wicked man in London. Nay, in England."

His chuckle surprised her.

"Well, you *did* marry the Devil of London." He rolled her onto her stomach. Then, without warning, he smacked her arse with his hand. The blow was not hard, but it made her squeak in surprise. He did it twice more, then stroked his palm soothingly over her bottom. It felt wonderful on the slightly stinging skin. Then she was turned on her back once more as he leaned over her.

"Too much?" he asked.

"No, my lord."

"Good." He pressed a heated kiss to her lips before he settled on his knees between her parted thighs. Then he lifted her hips, bringing her close to his lap but lifting her up enough that she could see her body. He tugged his trousers down, and his erection jutted toward her.

"Watch while I claim you," he ordered. There was a growl in his voice, a hint of the animal just beneath his skin that made her shiver in anticipation. He guided his shaft into her.

"Bloody Christ, you're tight." He pushed deeper and deeper into her. She watched in aroused fascination as they joined completely.

He began to thrust into her until they both made soft sounds at the back of their throats as their bodies joined over and over again. "Don't look away. Don't shut your eyes." The muscles of his chest and arms bunched as he pumped into her, and she couldn't look away, even if she wanted to. Her dark god of the underworld was owning her, body and soul. When their eyes met, she saw in that blinding instant as they came apart at the same time that she owned him too.

Hours later, Perdita lay on top of Vaughn, her legs now tangled with his, their bodies damp, and his slowly measured breathing, that of a man almost asleep, was comforting.

"It wasn't too much?" he asked.

She lifted her face to rest her chin on his chest. "No. It was perfect."

The boyish grin she adored was back. He toyed with a lock of her hair, spooling it around one of his fingers.

"A man could get spoiled having you for a wife."

"Indeed. I am wonderful," she agreed, biting back a smile.

"Cheeky little chit." He slapped her buttocks with his free hand, and she hissed. He had shown her his dark desires tonight, and she had discovered that hers matched his.

This beautiful, mysterious man loves me. He excites me. He makes me feel alive.

She kissed his chest and laid her head back down.

"Tell me we shall always be like this."

"It will always be like this. Except for, of course, when the children are old enough to sneak out of the nursery to find us. It will be even more fun evading the scamps to get a moment alone." He laughed, the rich sound rumbling deep from his chest.

"You want children?"

"More than anything, except for you."

She held on to him even tighter. "I'm glad of that."

He nuzzled her cheek and placed a kiss on her temple. "Are you truly happy to be my wife?"

She lifted her head again. "Infinitely so. And you? Are you happy to be my husband?"

His eyes were serious. "I am. There is something indescribable about the joy of sharing myself with you, of letting you into my heart. It was frightening at first, but now I can't imagine a day without you."

"So you love me?" She tried to sound teasing, but she had to hear the words from him.

"I do. I love you to distraction, to the depths of my soul and beyond."

"I love you too. My white knight." She brushed a hand over his chest. She'd come to realize that a man in perfect shining armor was a man who'd never been tested. Vaughn, in his tarnished armor, had proven how strong his mettle truly was more than once, and he loved her in ways she'd never dreamed of.

She slid up a few inches to kiss him, knowing that she had found love at last. It was on his lips, on his tongue, and in the way he held her. She knew snow was falling outside tonight and whispered a silent prayer of thanks for the gift of loving someone who loved her in return. It was the sort of miracle she had long given up hope on ever having.

Christmas, after all, was a season for hope, for miracles, for faith, and for love unending.

Wait! I know what you're thinking the book is over...but

please keep reading for just a few more pages. I've got some important info here in case you decide you love my books so you'll want to keep reading. *grins

You've just read the 3rd book in the Seduction series. The other books in the series are *The Duelist's Seduction,* and the upcoming book 2 *The Rakehell's Seduction.* Stay tuned for the 4th book in the series The Gentleman's Seduction coming soon!

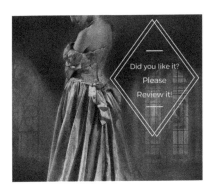

Want three free romance novels? Fill out the form at the bottom of this link and you'll get an email from me with details to collect your free reads!

Claim your free book now at: http://laurensmithbooks.com/free-books-and-newsletter/, follow me on twitter at @LSmithAuthor, or like my Facebook page at https://www.facebook.com/LaurenDianaSmith. I share upcoming book news, snippets and cover reveals plus PRIZES!

Reviews help other readers find books. I appreciate

all reviews, whether positive or negative. If one of my books spoke to you, please share!

WANT TO READ THE FIRST CHAPTER OF ANY OF MY BOOKS to see if you like it? Check out my Wattpad.com page where I post the first chapter of every book including ones not yet released! To start reading visit: https://www.wattpad.com/user/LaurenSmithAuthor.

IF YOU'D LIKE TO READ THE FIRST THREE CHAPTERS FROM *The Duelist's Seduction,* the first book in this series, please turn the page.

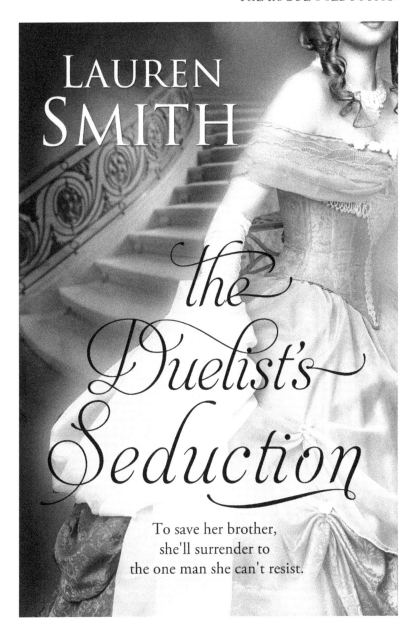

LAUREN SMITH

the Duelist's Seduction

To save her brother,
she'll surrender to
the one man she can't resist.

THE DUELIST'S SEDUCTION

CHAPTER 1

The predawn sky shone brightly with flickering stars as Helen Banks readied herself for the duel. Her hair was coiled and pinned tightly against her head, concealing its thick mass and giving her a boyish look—a disguise she prayed would last. Checking the black mask covering her face, she resumed walking. She took a deep, steadying breath as she adjusted her breeches and the black coat she'd pinched from her brother's wardrobe.

The open field near the spa city of Bath was quiet. Two coaches waited in the distance along the roadside, and ahead of her, two men waited, watching her approach. Not even a breeze dared rustle the knee-high grass as Helen walked up to her enemy and his second. Both men also wore masks to conceal their identities should someone witness the illegal duel. The paling skies played with the retreating shadows of night, lending a melancholy air to the moment she stopped inches from the men.

"You are late, Mr. Banks," the taller of the two men announced coldly.

With his broad shoulders and muscular body, Gareth Fairfax cut an imposing figure. He seemed perpetually tense, as though ready to strike out at anyone who might offend him. Dark hair framed his chiseled features, and the eyes that glowered from between the spaces of his mask were a fathomless blue. They were the sort of eyes a woman lost herself in, like gazing into a dark pool of water that seemed to sink endlessly, drawing her in until she can't find her way back to the surface. She recognized the sensual, full lips, now thinned by anger, and the gleam of his eyes on her. She was never more thankful that the early morning's pale light did not expose her as being a woman.

Helen hated knowing that even now, faced with possible death at his hands, she still desired him. Having seen him from afar over the past few months, she'd been enchanted. Gareth—for that was the way she'd dreamt about him, not as Mr. Fairfax—had a way about him, an animal magnetism that drew her in, with his smoky gaze and relaxed movements. Sin personified—she'd once heard a woman describe him thus at a dance and it was true. Even angels would be tempted to stray to hell for one glance, one lingering, seductive look. He smiled so rarely, she'd glimpsed it but twice in the months she'd seen him. Both times it had fairly knocked her off her feet with the sheer force of its power.

He'd never noticed her at the social engagements. She had stood close to the wall, quiet and lost in dreams as she watched him through her heavy lashes. Foolish, too, she knew, to look at him and feel such hunger for the things his brooding demeanor promised. He had passed her by on numerous occasions, but his head never turned and his eyes never alighted on her. Even now, as she stood before him, ready to die at his hands, she knew he thought her to be her twin brother, Martin.

If he ever discovered she was a woman, he would be appalled and furious. Especially given that she was only dueling him to save her brother's life.

She briefly studied her opponent's second. He was just as tall, his features nearly as striking as Gareth's.

Helen choked down a shaky breath. "I was waylaid." She prayed her voice sounded gruff and masculine.

Gareth's eyes were dark orbs, burning with thinly controlled anger. He shifted restlessly on his feet, his imposing form momentarily revealed by the dark blue coat that contoured to his shape.

"Is this your second?" His growl sent shivers down her spine as his glaze flicked to the squat man in his mid-thirties standing behind her. She glanced over her shoulder, widening her eyes in silent encouragement for her second to come closer.

"I am," Mr. Rodney Bennett replied and bowed.

"Mr. Banks, I am Mr. Ambrose Worthing," Gareth's second announced politely.

Well, finally someone was acting like a gentleman. "Mr. Worthing," Helen said, making sure to keep her voice low. "Allow me to introduce my second, Mr. Rodney Bennett."

Bennett passed by Helen, and he and Worthing shook hands. Bennett offered the pistols to Worthing for inspection. Since Gareth and Worthing had not brought the weapons, that duty fell to her as the challenged party. As the two men drew apart from her and Gareth, she tried not to stare at him. He was impossibly handsome, in that dark, mysterious sort of way that a woman simply couldn't ignore. Like gazing upon a visage of an angry god, all fire and might, ready to burn her to ash with passion.

Her opponent glowered at her. "I suppose I should trust that you've not tampered with my pistol?"

His icy tone made her bristle with indignation. "You have my word it shoots fair," Helen snapped. The nerve of the man to accuse her of cheating!

"Your word? We would not be here if I could trust your word. A man who does not honor his debts may not find it necessary to honor the rules of a duel," Gareth retorted.

She wanted to scream. Her fists clenched at her sides. Her nails dug painfully into her palms as she struggled to calm down. She wanted to throttle her brother, whose rash and inconsiderate behavior had gotten her into this mess.

"Easy, Fairfax. Both pistols appear to be in working order," Worthing announced as he and Bennett rejoined them.

Helen breathed a sigh of relief as Bennett resumed his position behind her. She'd paid him the last bit of money she'd had for him to appear as her second. She didn't really know the man, having only met him briefly when she'd had to drag her brother away from the card tables a few nights ago. When she first approached Bennett with her plan, he had tried to talk her out of it, but when she offered money, he couldn't refuse and had agreed to help her take her brother's place in the duel. Even though he was a gentleman, the gambler inside him craved any bit of money he could get his hands on to return to the tables. She was lucky he hadn't gambled away his pair of pistols, or else she would have been completely humiliated to turn up at a duel without weapons.

"Now," Mr. Worthing said, "before we settle this, is it possible that you and Mr. Banks can reconcile the dispute?"

Helen started to nod, wanting desperately to find a way to settle the problem without bloodshed, but Gareth spoke up, stilling the bobbing of her head.

"Mr. Banks has run up a debt to me of over a thousand pounds. He has not been able to pay it back to me over the last three months. Furthermore, he created an additional liability of five hundred pounds last evening when he played with money he did not have."

Helen swallowed hard, a painful lump in her throat choking her. *Martin, you damned fool...*

"Why did you accept his vouchers then?" Rodney spoke up. "I saw you agree to play with him. You didn't have to."

"Banks had money on him. I assumed he'd replenished his funds and would settle his debts to me." Gareth shot a withering look in Helen's direction. "Shooting him will be a bonus."

Helen held his stare for a moment, feeling the regret deep in her belly that she hadn't known better than to trust her twin brother—too childish for a gentleman of one-and-twenty—to be more responsible. Instead of helping to secure her a position as a governess—their finances dim after the death of their parents and no good marriages likely—he had been losing what meager fortune they had to men like Gareth Fairfax, who had plenty to spare.

A man who would now take her life as payment for a debt she didn't owe. But what else could she do? She couldn't let Martin die. A man had options to survive, a woman did not, at least not one that wouldn't make her despise herself for the rest of her life.

Her memory of the previous night was tinged with fury and disappointment in Martin. Her heart had plummeted into the pit of her stomach when she'd retired for the evening and found his room empty. All of her hopes were dashed the moment she'd learned he'd gone back to the gambling tables.

She'd hidden in the shadows outside the gambling hell, trying not to be seen by anyone passing by. The smell of alcohol stung her nose, and the raucous laughter echoing from the entrance sent chills of trepidation down her spine. It would ruin her completely if she were witnessed outside such an establishment. Bennett had promised to bring Martin out to her, but when Martin emerged, he was being roughly hauled out by a dark-haired gentleman, a man she recognized, a man she'd admired for the last few months from afar.

"I'll honor my debt to you, Mr. Fairfax," Martin had drunkenly promised, over and over again.

Gareth Fairfax, following behind her brother, grabbed Martin by his coat collar and rammed him up against the stone wall of the nearest building.

"Honor your debt? With what, pray tell? You played that last hand without a shilling to your name," Gareth growled. "You haven't even redeemed your vowels for the last few times of play. I demand satisfaction." Gareth released Martin, who sagged against the wall in defeat.

Martin's head had bowed wearily in submission. "Name the location and time."

"There is a field two miles east of the Crow tavern. Be there tomorrow morning one hour before the sun rises. There is a full moon. That will do. I have no intention of being chased out of the country because of you. Bring a second and your choice of weapon." Gareth had stalked off, leaving Martin alone. He shook his head as though to clear it, and with steps none too steady, started walking in Helen's direction.

When he passed by the alcove where she was hiding, she stepped out and struck her brother as hard as she could on the shoulder. Her anger flared. "You fool! That man is going to kill you!"

"Helen?" Martin said in shock. "What the bloody hell are you doing here? You should be at home."

She narrowed her eyes. "I had hoped to get you out of that place before you lost everything we have. It seems I am too late." She hoped her accusation stung. It was nothing less than he deserved.

Martin glanced at her. Under the glow of the streetlight, she saw guilt deepening the color of his lightly tanned skin.

"I'm sorry, Helen... I thought I could win back our money and more." His tone was apologetic, but it lost some of its effect when he hiccupped.

Helen waited for Martin to say something, but he did not. Her voice shook with a mixture of fear and fury. "I forbid you to go tomorrow morning. What will I do if you die, Martin?"

"I won't die," he replied sullenly. "I'm a crack shot. I stand an even chance."

"An even chance of what?" Helen nearly shrieked. "Killing a man and being made to leave the country? Do you even care what would happen to me without you?"

"Is that all I am? Someone to take care of you?" he shot back.

Helen's eyes burned with tears and she threw her arms around her brother. "No, you fool. I love you. I don't want to lose you. How can you not understand that? After mama and papa..." her voice broke, but she forced herself to continue. "I *cannot* lose you, too."

"Well it doesn't matter, does it? I have to meet Fairfax tomorrow." Her brother's mouth assumed a mulish cast, and she knew it would do no good to argue with him.

He was as stubborn as their father had been. They did not speak the rest of the way back to their lodgings, but Helen's mind worked frantically. She loved Martin, he was her other half, as any true twins were. She had to save him, had to find a way to fix what he'd done, or if not fix it, then sacrifice herself for him. It was the only way. One of them had to survive, and he stood a better chance on his own than she did.

She'd formed a plan. She and her brother were almost the same height, and their build was similar enough that as children they'd often been mistaken for one another. If she dressed as a male, could she pass for him? When her brother woke up early the next morning to prepare for the duel, Helen took her father's cane, one of the last pieces of his belongings they hadn't sold, and knocked Martin out. She dressed in an extra set of his clothes and locked Martin in his room.

It was a simple solution to a complex problem. Martin was a man and could live on without her. It was easier for men to make their way in the world. A penniless young lady with no family and no connections had no such luck. The best she could hope for was a position as a governess or companion, and without references, those positions were almost impossible to find. The only other possibility was one she would not consider. Even being a maid would be better than selling her body.

And that was how she'd ended up on this field, facing the one man she'd dreamt about dancing with and knowing she never would. A man above her in station, money, and power. A man with secretive smiles, and a soft, low seductive voice, surrounded by rumors whispered behind fans in the assembly halls of how he must make a good lover. She would never know if any of it was true now, not that she'd ever had a chance to earn his interest at the balls before.

Mr. Worthing cleared his throat. "Fairfax, would you be willing to work with Mr. Banks?"

Even in the pre-dawn light, Helen could see Gareth's face darken in anger. "I would find a way to repay you, sir," Helen said quickly. Like a man about to be hanged, she clung to the last few minutes she'd have of life, even if it meant lying. There would be no way to repay him, of course, but she had to try. She had to hope her opponent still had some kindness and would delay her demise a few precious seconds.

"You've had weeks to repay me, and I've not seen one shilling. There will be no settlement." Gareth's tone was quieter, almost resigned, as he checked his pistol, flicked his glance at her, and then nodded to Worthing.

So much for compassion. The last hope of her survival had died with his curt nod. Helen's heart kicked into a faster pace. Her fear created a bitter, metallic taste in her mouth as she realized she'd been hoping the duel wouldn't actually happen. But of course it would. Men like Gareth valued honor, and her brother had none. This duel was unavoidable.

Worthing sighed heavily, apparently convinced there was no turning back. He and Bennett walked several yards away to watch the proceedings.

She and Gareth were alone, closer than they'd ever been before tonight. How many times had she peered through the crowds of dancers in the assembly rooms and watched him dance with other women, wishing she was the one that close to him? Now here she was, close enough to dance, but it was to be a dance of death. A hollow ache filled her chest at the thought, and a whisper of fear made her heart shudder behind her ribs.

I don't want to die, but what choice is there?

The faint breeze brought his scent of sandalwood and the faintest hint of horses and leather to her nose. The aroma made her homesick for the stables in her parents' home in the country, a home she and Martin had to sell in order to survive. The pistol grew heavier in her hands, the wood and metal sinking into her palm with force as she curled her fingers around it more securely. The silence and her fear made it all suddenly unbearable.

"Very well," Helen growled, losing her ability to remain calm and still any longer. The only way to quell her fear was to embrace her anger. "Name your distance, sir." If she was to die, let it be done already. This waiting and delay was eating away at her courage.

"Thirty paces." Gareth replied after a moment's hesitation. He seemed to be peering at her more sharply, as though something had attracted his attention. His usually sensual full lips were thinned into a frown. Surely he couldn't have realized she wasn't Martin... She had to distract him.

"Thirty." She nodded, relieved to know it helped mask the way her entire body shook with a new wave of fear. She'd never imagined facing death like this, especially not at the hands of a man she desired. Fate was cruel. "Let us finish this." She turned her back to Gareth and waited.

He closed the distance between them and put his back up against hers. She shivered at the sudden warmth of his body against hers, his backside pressed ever so lightly against her lower back. His clothing whispered against hers, like a strange sort of dance, and then Gareth moved away as Mr. Worthing began to count. She began to mark the paces as well, trying to ignore the roaring of blood in her ears and the realization that each step brought her that much closer to her death.

When Mr. Worthing called out to halt Helen and Gareth at thirty paces, they turned to face each other. The velvet skies were paler now, as though the stars had blinked, closing their celestial eyes to miss the grisly scene about to unfold below. Helen saw Gareth turn sideways and raise his arm. She copied the movement, aiming her pistol at Gareth's chest. The pale moonlight glinted off the gun in his hand as he trained it on her chest. Her entire body started to shake as instinctive fear took over. There was a pistol pointed at her heart. Her hand trembled, the barrel of her own gun wavering. She wouldn't shoot him, there was no doubt of that.

"One," Worthing called out. "Two..."

Helen's eyes shot up from Gareth's pistol to his face. He was far enough away to appear more a shadow dressed in black with glowing eyes than the man she'd longed to share the secrets of her heart with.

"Three—"

Her finger clenched around the trigger and she fired without meaning to. Her shot went wide, grazing Gareth's shoulder. He flinched but did not fire. Blood sprayed along his shirt, nearly black in the distance. She gasped and sucked in a violent breath, her vision spinning momentarily.

Horrified she had actually hit him, she dropped her pistol and it landed with a *thunk* in the grass. She ran over to him, reaching out to check the damage.

His dark eyes flashed in surprise as she clutched his arm and examined the wound.

"Oh Good Heavens!" she cried. "The one time I fire one of these stupid things..."

By the time she realized her higher feminine tone had betrayed her, Gareth, in one swift motion, had dropped his own pistol and grabbed her by the arm, dragging her against him. He ripped the mask from her face. Her pins sprung loose from the rough movement, releasing the bound up hair. The loose waves dropped down against her shoulders, the soft strands caressing her cheeks as she ducked her head, hiding her face from him. Gareth's look of rage turned to sheer astonishment.

"Where is Martin Banks?" His voice was rough and low. "And who the devil are you?"

His grip was too strong and Helen started to lose feeling in her arm. "Please, you're hurting me," she gasped.

Her plea went ignored. He didn't release his hold on her, but he lightened his hold so it was no longer bruising.

"Where is Banks?" He shook her and shouted angrily.

"Unconscious, in our lodgings." Helen tried to break free, but his iron grip held her fast. "I could not let you kill him." His eyes sharpened at her defiance.

Worthing and Bennett ran towards them.

"A woman?" Worthing called out in surprise. "Really, Fairfax... you should have told me," When Worthing strode over to her and Gareth, his eyes shifted between them as they stood locked together by Gareth's vice-like grip.

"Let go of her, Fairfax," Worthing slowly reached out and pried her loose from Gareth's arms.

Gareth batted Worthing's protective arm aside and gripped her by the shoulders, rattling her. "Who are you?" he snarled, his white, even teeth shining in the dim light. "Why are you here in Banks's place?"

"Let go of her," Bennett growled and moved a step toward Gareth. Worthing lifted a hand to stay Bennett and tried once more to intervene, but Gareth dragged her away from Worthing's reach.

"Well? Answer me! I have no intention of hurting you, but I will get answers." His angry gaze bore into her like a hot poker.

Helen bit back furious tears. "I'm his sister. He is my only family." Her body started that awful shaking again, this time from the shock of being alive and unhurt. "I would be utterly alone should he perish."

"Don't you dare cry. I'll not be moved by a woman's tears," he threatened, but his grip softened immediately, belaying whatever cruelty hung in his words.

"Fairfax," Worthing cautioned at the same time Bennett said, "Release her!"

Everything happened so fast, it was almost a blur. Bennett tried to step between Gareth and Helen but stumbled back as Gareth pummeled him in the stomach. Helen screamed and struck out at Gareth, slapping him hard across the face. Worthing dove out of the way as Gareth tackled Helen to the ground. Bennett tried once more to rescue her but was felled by another punch from Gareth.

"Damnit Fairfax, hold off!" Worthing knelt by the unconscious Bennett.

"Keep that bloody fool away from me. I'm not going to hurt her," Gareth growled. "I want her to answer me." He was gazing down at her, a new light in his eyes, a light that was less dangerous, or perhaps more so, but in a different way. As though he was appraising her, or assessing her value, the way a man studies a good piece of horseflesh at the market when selecting a ride. It was not the gaze of a man who would strike out at her or wound her.

Helen gasped, struggling beneath Gareth's body. She wasn't afraid now, but more angry at the way he had manhandled her. He sat back on his heels, his knees on either side of her hips, still pinning her to the ground. His chest heaved with panting breaths, and his palms fell to his thighs.

She attempted to raise her hips but couldn't budge. "Please, let me go." He tensed at her movement, his fingers digging into his thighs.

"Whatever shall I do with you, Miss Banks?" Gareth's breath evened out. "We have ourselves quite the problem."

"Fairfax..." Worthing's tone held an edge of warning. Gareth ignored him, a calculating gleam in his eyes.

Swallowing hard, she met his gaze as evenly as she could.

"I have a proposal for you, Miss Banks," Gareth said peacefully, but the shadows in his gaze made her wary. One of his hands drifted to her hair, allowing her blonde curls to cascade around and through his fingers. He suddenly smiled, taking one lock and twining it around his index finger, his eyes meeting hers. "If you come to my home with me, I will forget the debts owed to me. Or I send you back to Bath, find that scoundrel you call a brother, and finish this duel properly."

Helen blinked. Go home with Gareth Fairfax? She may have been an innocent, but she knew that if he were to take her to his home, she would be compromised—ruined for marriage. *Certainly ruined for any other man.* A blush warmed her whole body just thinking of what he would do to her if she agreed. *Ruined.* Part of her was filled with a secret, dark curiosity. Would he seduce her? She should have been more frightened by the fact that she was curious enough to wonder what it would be like to be with him. Women seemed to like seduction under the right circumstances. A spark of heat shot through her body at the thought of Gareth willfully seducing her.

"If I agree to go with you, what would you do with me?" The words came out thick, her tongue seemingly unable to form the words as she dared to ask about his intentions.

He didn't speak for a long moment. Instead he rubbed his thumb and forefinger against the lock of her hair. Finally, he let the loose curl drop and settled his hand back on his thigh, shifting his hips slightly. It pressed him harder against her and her own body flashed with a strange, queer sort of fire.

"You can settle your brother's debts to me one way or another." His tone was black as midnight, dark as sin, and rather than frighten her, it made her tremble with longing. She had heard enough women speak behind closed doors at the balls to know that what could happen between a man and woman in bed could be pleasurable for both parties.

Worthing stood up and eyed his friend. "Fairfax, you can't just take her home."

Gareth's eyes searched her face and settled on her lips. "She's already said that Banks is her only relative, Worthing. No one will miss her. It's her choice. She's free to leave, or she can come with me and save her brother's life."

"You can't be serious. The young woman was only defending her brother. You cannot ruin a lady over that."

She watched the exchange, wondering why Worthing was so ready to defend her.

"Well, Miss Banks?" He continued to study her, his body keeping hers trapped as though there really was no option but to accept him. "Make your choice. Dawn is chasing us, and I, for one, don't wish to be here when the sun fully rises." He leaned down and whispered in her ear. "I promise to take good care of you and give you so much pleasure you might feel you'll die from it." The feel of his warm breath against the sensitive shell of her ear sent sparks shooting down her spine and she tensed.

Helen gazed up at him, desire running riotously through her

body, and her mind whispered dark suggestions, borne of long years of need for things she barely understood. This was a chance to taste temptation, to be with a handsome man and know passion. There would never be love, she knew that, but passion might prove a memory worth having, especially with a man like him. Did she dare, though? Any chance of marrying, having children, would be at an end, and if anyone discovered where she was, her reputation would be ruined. Even obtaining employment as a maid would become difficult. Yet Martin would be safe, and he may yet find a way to make a living and support himself and her. It was a feeble hope, but that would be the only future she could hope for. Gareth had said he'd treat her well. Really, what choice did she have?

"Yes, Mr. Fairfax. I'll go with you."

The finality behind her words was heavy, and Gareth tensed above her, eyes widening. He hadn't expected her to agree? A ripple of power flowed through her. She liked surprising him. He scanned her face again, his eyes darkening, but not with anger. This time it was something else that gleamed in their depths.

Worthing moved towards them, one hand raised. "Now, hold on Fairfax. I must insist you think this through."

Gareth slid off Helen and grabbed her arms, pulling her onto her feet. She barely heard the men arguing. All she was aware of was Gareth's hands on her body as he lifted her up and into him, letting her lean against his arm, as though aware she needed help to stand. The muscles beneath his shirt were taut and large. Heat emanated against her palms when she rested them briefly against his chest as she finally pushed away to stand on her own. He kept hold of her wrists, though, despite the tentative tug she gave to be released.

"I'm not in the mood for a lecture, Worthing. You take care of that...fellow. I will bring Miss Banks to my house. After you've seen to him, you can come and rescue the woman if you feel you must." There was a mixture of amusement and warning in Gareth's tone that confused Helen. "Provided you can convince her to go."

She tugged at her wrists, still trapped by his hands. Even

though she'd agreed to accompany him, the fact that he still held her caused an unsettling heat to stir between her thighs. Helen clenched her legs together, desperate to stop the sensation. She tugged her hands again.

"Stop that," he growled and started walking.

Helen obeyed instantly. He was too strong for her to resist, so she followed, struggling to keep pace with his long-legged strides. They crossed the field and moved in the direction of the road where Helen had been dropped off by the hired conveyance. Gareth's coach stood waiting. The driver jumped down to lower the steps, and Gareth pulled her against him as he lifted her into the vehicle. Once they were settled inside, sharing the same seat, he shouted an order to the driver and the coach jerked forward. She rubbed her wrists, wondering if they'd bruise, and tried not to look at him. She failed.

He turned his head towards the window and away from her, his expression cool and unemotional. She couldn't believe that he actually desired her. Not when he'd had his pick of women in Bath. Compared to those other ladies, Helen knew she didn't measure up, so Gareth's choice made little sense.

"Why did you want me to come with you?" Helen dared herself to ask when the silence had stretched too long between them.

He fixed his cold gaze on her once more. "Because your brother must learn that his actions have consequences. If I have you, it will cause trouble for him. He'll have to find a way to marry you off after I'm done, not an easy task for a man with a ruined sister. It won't amount to the money he won off me, but it will be some measure of revenge."

Helen shut her eyes for a few minutes, jostled by the battering of the coach wheels on the rough road. Her stomach roiled with nausea. So he didn't desire her. Using her was only about revenge. Disappointment weighed her shoulders down, pressing on her chest. She sucked in a much needed breath. It was a cruel sort of feeling to go from believing she was desired to learning her seduction and ruination were merely payback for her brother's carelessness. In that moment, Helen felt very small and alone, uncared for, and unloved in the worst way. The most awful part was the way it seemed to take the wind from her sails. All of her high spirits, even the angry ones, were dashed upon the rocks. Would it be worth it —going with him, exploring her own passions—even when he might not feel them in return? There seemed no ready answer.

When she opened her eyes, he was staring at her still. This time, his eyes were more curious than cold. He had a beautiful profile—strong and straight like the statue Michelangelo's David. How many hours at the balls and soirees had she spent studying each feature of him? Too many. As a wallflower, she'd had endless hours to memorize him, fantasize about him. What would she have said if only he'd asked her to dance once? A girlish dream, one that now lay dead in the field they'd just left. She would never be that woman, the one that handsome men would ask to dance or pay court to. She was just another woman who would go without love, and now, without marriage. Still, his face would haunt her forever. She could recall each line, each shape of his features...draw them perfectly from her dreams, if needed.

"What is your given name?" His question drew her from her thoughts.

"Helen," she replied, her eyes drawn to the curve of his lips as he smiled.

"Like fair Helen of Troy...do you bring ruin to my kingdom?" he mused, more to himself than to her.

"I only wished to save my brother's life. Had I died, he would be no worse off than before. But had our positions been reversed... I would have no one to protect me."

"A tragedy to any woman," Gareth agreed.

At least he understood. She had no money and no friends. Without her brother, she'd be lost to decent society. She might have to sell herself to survive. Helen's lips quivered at that thought —to be so desperate for food that she would... A dark thought trespassed in her mind. Was agreeing to Gareth's proposal any better? She shivered at where such ideas led.

"Calm yourself." There was an underlying callousness to his words that rekindled her fire. "I'll not hurt you. No woman has ever left my bed with any complaints." His tone was layered with smug satisfaction. He leaned back in the coach seat, stretching out long, muscled legs, and crossing his boots at the ankles. She was reminded of a tomcat merely biding his time to make his move on the unsuspecting female cat he planned to mate with. She was the female cat in this scenario, and it did not make her feel safe at all. What little she'd heard of him from other ladies in society was that he wasn't rumored to be a cruel man. That was her only solace —that he wouldn't truly harm her.

The ride was long. Helen couldn't help but wonder what type of house he had, to live so far from Bath. At some point, fatigue overcame her. She didn't want to show weakness in front of him, but when her eyelids kept falling shut, she knew she was lost. Her head fell against Gareth's shoulder as she drifted off to sleep. She woke a while later when the pattern of the horses' hooves changed and the wheels slowed to a halt. Still drowsy, she raised her head from his shoulder, blushed when she realized he was staring at her, and scooted a little ways away. Running her hands through her hair, she tried to tame the wild waves.

Gareth opened the coach door and helped her out. He kept a gentle but firm grip on her arm as they walked up a set of stone steps. A matronly woman with graying hair waited for them just inside the door.

"Good, evening, Mary. Prepare a room for Miss Banks. She will be our guest for a time," Gareth said to the woman.

Mary's eyes widened in surprise, but she did not question him.

Helen gulped. How long was her stay to be? Gareth had not given any indication of its duration.

"Mr. Fairfax, how long do you intend to keep me here?" She held her breath so long her lungs burned.

He did not look at her as they followed Mary. "As long as necessary. I'll likely tire of you in a few weeks."

His words were a slap to her soul and she flinched.

Mary departed, winding her way up the grand staircase to prepare a room for her. Helen was once more alone with the brooding and frightening Gareth Fairfax. He still held her arm as he escorted her to a mahogany and wine colored drawing room where a warm fire was lit. A pair of deep-backed chairs faced the fire, and Helen was pushed toward the one furthest from the door. Gareth took the other, his chair slightly angled toward her.

The dimness of the room, lit by only a few candles, and the roaring fire's warmth was seductive and inviting, like a strange sort of dream. Perhaps she was dreaming, and none of this was real. She'd wake soon and prepare a meager breakfast for Martin and... but she knew the truth. This was all too real and she was very vulnerable. A little tremor stole through her arms and chest.

"You find yourself in an unfortunate predicament, Miss Banks. I owe your brother a bullet. The duel was not finished. I've taken you, by your choice, in his place." His eyes reflected the fire's glow, wild and untamable.

Helen could not respond. Fascination rippled through her as she studied his lips, his eyes, his dark hair that gleamed in the firelight. He was a devil, but a handsome one, and his harsh gaze made her heart beat rapidly. It was madness to long for his seduction, to pray for it with every breath. Surely the fires of hell awaited her for her thoughts.

"My temper has cooled. I have no interest in shooting anyone at the moment, but your brother owes me a great deal of money." She'd expected him to be more businesslike, but there was a pensive musing to his voice that drew her in...made her wonder what he was truly thinking.

He seemed to be watching her for some reaction, but Helen did not understand the weight his words carried.

"We have no way of repaying you," she replied gravely. "I used the last bit of money I had to secure Mr. Bennett's support for the duel. I had hoped to gain a position as governess...that is, before Martin quarreled with you. If you give me time, I'm sure I could think of a way to settle our debt."

"Would you deny me, should I demand a different form of payment? It is why I brought you here, after all." The question was delivered very slowly and deliberately. His gaze raked up and down her body more savagely than she thought a look ever could. Helen paled, her earlier suspicion had been right.

"What would you have me do while I'm here?" Her words came out a strangled whisper. She knew what he would say, hoped breathlessly that he would, as dangerous and foolish as it was to wish for him to desire her.

Gareth stood up and, in one elegant move, came around behind her chair, his hands falling lightly onto her shoulders. He slowly swept her long hair away from her neck, baring part of her throat. One of his fingers drew a lazy pattern on her skin, teasing the tiny hairs which rose at his touch, and she shivered. He bent over the back of the chair, his lips brushing her ear as he spoke, stirring her senses.

"Remain here, at my beck and call, as a companion of sorts." He caught her chin with his hand and gently turned her face towards his, his lips so close to hers she could almost feel them. She swallowed uncomfortably as her mouth grew dry. "When I tire of you, I shall return you to Bath, and your brother's debt will be fully paid." His hands slid down her shoulders, along the sides of her arms. For the first time in her life, she was torn, her mind and heart were warning her against him, but her body was enticed by the slightest touch of his hands, the brush of his lips. Her face flushed with heat as he kissed her softly below the ear.

"And if I refuse?" The room slowly spun, and her head filled with a strange buzzing. Her skin tingled beneath his touch. She ought to refuse. Staying here would ruin her respectability...the last thing she had left that couldn't be bought or destroyed, except it seemed, by this dark, brooding man. Yet she'd chosen, as he'd reminded her, to come here voluntarily. She couldn't lie to herself. She'd known of his intentions to bed her from the start, but she longed to test him, to see what he would say if she pretended to change her mind.

"Then I lock you in a room here and ride straight to Bath to find your brother." Gareth's words were sinister, but his voice was as smooth as honey. Helen's eyelashes fluttered down against her cheeks as she fought to hide her emotions. It wouldn't be wise for him to know his power over her...how easily he enthralled her with the carnal promise in his eyes. He came back around to stand in front of her.

"So, Miss Banks, will you accept?" He crossed his arms in front of his chest, looking down at her imperiously.

Helen rose from her chair, glad for her height. She needed to be his equal if she was going to accept this bargain. He didn't tower over her as much as he would have other women. For a long moment, she gazed back at him, weighing her options. Ruin herself and save her brother? Or save herself and sign her brother's death sentence. Sadly, the choice was easier than it ought to have been. She would do *anything* to protect Martin. And she'd also not refuse herself this one chance to know passion.

"I accept, so long as you vow that my brother will not be harmed and his debt to you will be satisfied." Her voice didn't waver.

Gareth nodded slowly. "I will honor those terms."

Helen held out a hand to shake upon it. "Then we have a bargain."

Gareth looked down at her hand, a slow smile spreading across his lips. He took her hand and before she could protest, he tugged her into his arms. It was her first kiss, and not at all what she had expected. This was no innocent meeting of lovers' lips. Gareth's mouth caught hers, moving in deep, teasing motions that sent shivers down her spine. One of his hands coiled in her hair, twining his fingers in her silky strands. He clenched, just enough to cause her to open her mouth wider in a gasp born of pleasure at the slight pain. He plundered her mouth, his tongue diving to mate with hers.

A throbbing pulse burst into life between her legs and her knees gave way, knocking against his. He wound an arm about her waist, holding her to him. Like a limp ragdoll, she surrendered to his amorous attentions, the sensations overwhelming and intoxicating. She wished she knew what to do—how to move her lips, where to place her hands—to please him in return.

His hand in her hair held her captive for his exploring mouth, which tasted her lips, her neck, her collarbone, and behind her ears. And then it was over. He spun her gently out of his grasp, grinning at her smugly.

"That is how we seal our bargain, my darling."

The glare she sent him only made him smile.

He gestured for her to follow him. "I'm sure Mary has prepared your chamber by now." Helen trailed behind him as they left the drawing room. An upstairs maid stood at the foot of the stairs, waiting.

"The lady's room is ready, sir," the ginger-haired maid bobbed in a shallow curtsey.

"Thank you, Mira. Which room is it?"

"The third guest room on the right, sir." The maid looked expectantly to Gareth.

"That will be all, Mira. Run along to bed."

Helen watched as the maid ducked back down the stairs and through a door that probably led to the servants' quarters. It took every ounce of her will not to call out for the maid to stay and not leave them alone. She wasn't afraid of him, but nerves made her shaky. There was so much about being with a man in bed that she didn't know. Any woman with good sense would be nervous about her first time, even though he'd assured her she would enjoy it. Gareth tugged Helen's hand, forcing her to follow him up the stairs and down the hall. He paused at the third room on the right, just as the maid had directed. The door stood open, the room ready for her.

It had a beautiful four-poster bed with velvet hangings and a ruby red coverlet. A thin white nightgown lay draped over the middle of the bed. Walking away from him, Helen picked the garment up, admiring its beautiful but simple design. She had never owned anything so fine in her life. Rather than bid her good-night, Gareth came into the room and shut the door. The snick of the door settling into the frame held a frightening finality. They were alone again. Helen backed away in fear, her heart racing. Did he mean to take her so soon?

I am not ready. I want him, but I am not prepared.

Gareth walked over to the armoire that faced the bed and tapped it lightly.

"There are gowns in here. They may not fit properly, but I will have my housekeeper send for ones that will. You may rest a while if you wish. Mary will be here to help you dress later in the morning. It has been some time since you've eaten, I assume. The servants will prepare whatever you wish after you've rested." He came back to her, cupping her chin, his voice gentler than it had been since they'd first met on the field for the duel.

"Th...thank you, Mr. Fairfax," Helen stammered, her body shaking slightly with fear.

She'd had such courage in the field, ready to face death for her brother, but this was so different. She'd come here, agreeing to be his mistress, in a fashion. She had little knowledge of the ways of men. Would he prepare her for their joining? Or would he be ruthless, take her hard, and not think a moment about her pleasure? The second the thought passed her mind, she shoved it aside. Helen had made a study of Gareth over the last few months, seen him interact with men and women, and she knew enough of reading a person's character to know he wouldn't hurt her. But he also wouldn't let her walk away from what she'd promised to give him.

"Mr. Fairfax—" she stammered.

"I give you leave to address me by my Christian name, Gareth." He smiled again, his eyes shining with hidden laughter. "You're afraid of me." He teased.

Helen clasped her shaking hands together. "Of course I am. You were going to shoot me. And now I'm here...unchaperoned in your house with the agreement between us that I share your bed.

I've never been with a man, and frankly, the prospect of it scares me a little. I would be a fool to not be a little afraid."

"You certainly are no fool. Feisty, but not foolish. A unique trait in a woman. You've no reason to fear me. There will be only pleasure between us." Gareth slowly reached out and captured her hips, his fingers digging for a better hold as he drew her against him. The smile that curved his lips heated her blood and sent her heart skittering. He rocked her into him, as though he meant to give her a gentle, teasing shake to cheer her up and relax her.

"Prepare yourself, Helen. I am going to kiss you again." And he did. A feathery brush of lips on lips. Helen's eyes drifted shut at the pleasurable sensation of his embrace.

The kiss changed, becoming slow and deep, his tongue easing between her lips. The sensation was strange, but Helen found herself kissing him back, her own tongue exploring him in turn. She was barely aware of him pushing her back against the bedpost until the wood dug between her shoulder blades. Gasping against him, she shuddered as he unbuttoned her breeches and slid his palm down her abdomen to part the thatch of pale curls between her legs. Gareth pinned her body with his, trapping her against the bedpost while using his hand to cup her mound. She tensed, gasping as he rubbed her with the heel of his hand. The rough pad of his thumb brushed her sensitive bud while another figure probed at the throbbing folds. She bit her lip, whimpering at the powerful zing of pleasure from his touch, and her body bucked forward. Was this how it really felt to be with a man? To feel the riotous waves of building excitement? She wanted more, so much more.

"Please!" Helen could barely form a coherent thought. His thumb tweaked her again, stronger this time, and a second finger joined the first, pushing deep into her tight sheath.

"You like this?" Gareth growled against her neck, taking tiny tastes of her skin as he slid his fingers in and out, thrusting in a slow, deliberate pattern designed to drive her mad.

Her answer was a plaintive moan. She wrapped her arms around his neck, clinging to him for support.

"Soon, I will taste you here," he pressed firmly on the bud, and the lightning flash of that touch exploded like a fire inside her.

"And I will take you here, hard and fast. Then so slow you will beg for mercy. And just when you drift off to sleep, I'll cover you again and thrust my cock so deep into you that you'll scream for more." As he spoke, his words were rough against her neck, tickling her skin, which was still damp from his kisses.

Helen gasped in breathless wonder as a powerful sensation spread through her, tingles, fire, and sparks alternating beneath her skin. Her knees knocked together as her legs gave out. His arms around her were the only thing keeping her upright. Gareth cupped her mound hard, holding her up as he continued to kiss her. She barely responded, too relaxed from the pleasure weighting her body with lethargy, so she merely consented to his rich plundering tongue. The fingers in her sheath withdrew, leaving her feeling strangely empty. But he moved his hand to her bottom, patting it softly as though to reward her for her inability to walk or talk. She knew she ought to have been indignant at his treatment of her, but she was too elated and drunk on the aftershocks of the explosion of sated desire which flashed and burned between her thighs.

He broke away when she started to seek his lips for another kiss. With a smirk of satisfaction, he left her alone in her bedchamber. She heard a click as something turned in the door. He had locked her in! She had agreed to stay here, but the sound of that lock turning infuriated her. She stumbled on weak legs to the door, tugging fiercely at the handle, which did not budge.

"Please... Gareth, let me out!" she called. "I said I would stay! Please!"

Silence.

He wanted her locked away. Why? Did he lie to her? Was he going to return to Bath, kill her brother, and return to take her to his bed? Surely, he couldn't be so cruel. Helen twisted at the knob again, hating that it didn't open, didn't budge an inch. She turned to look about the room. The thick paned windows weren't the type to open, and she wouldn't be able to break through it fast enough to escape without waking the entire house with the noise.

Helen choked down a panicked sob and abandoned the door. She prayed with every bit of her heart that Gareth hadn't decided to return to Bath and kill Martin. Maybe he had another reason for locking her in, even if she couldn't fathom why.

"Gareth, please..." she whispered into the wood of the door. Still silence. A wave of exhaustion swept her with such force that her head was too thick with a fog that made it hard to think. Gareth wouldn't kill Martin. He'd made a promise to her. Tomorrow she would demand to know why he'd locked her away tonight, and she would not let him do it again.

She retrieved the nightgown and, after a moment, prepared for bed. When she climbed between the sheets, she buried her face in the soft mound of pillows. Hot tears leaked from the corner of her eyes, soaking the cloth. Helen fought off the drowning despair that swamped her, but she couldn't hold long. Between this morning's near disaster on the field and the way Gareth had so coldly abandoned her just now, she was completely confused, both mentally and physically, and her crying grew harsh and ragged.

What had she done? She was trapped here by her own foolishness. And Martin... Would he try to find her? Would Gareth kill him if he came here? It was a long while before Helen cried herself into a deep sleep, unaware of the shadow that lingered outsider her door, listening to her weep.

THE DUELIST'S SEDUCTION

CHAPTER 2

Gareth listened to Helen tug on the locked door handle. He was on the verge of going to his own chambers when she began to cry. He froze mid-step. It was such a quiet, sweet, sad noise. It reminded him of a time when he'd captured and caged a wild thrush.

The little bird had been stunned at first, quiet and unsure, before it began to sing a sad little song, a plea of mercy. The thrush had only lasted a few weeks in a cage before its chirps lost their wild charms. Gareth knew that he had to release the bird if he ever wished to hear its song again, but the fear of letting go struck him deep. He had worked hard to make the bird his own, and he didn't want to release his hard won prize. But he knew with certainty that the bird would lose its song. Finally, he'd had to set it free. The memory of letting it go was burned into his heart. As the cage latch sprang open and the bird shot out of its prison, it fluttered away, and Gareth's heart fell. He would never hear it sing again.

But a minute later, he heard the distant trill slowly growing louder. The little thrush had returned. It perched on the edge of the garden wall, chattering away as though it had never been held prisoner. Perhaps Helen was like the thrush...needed to be kept caged for a time before he would release her, and maybe then she would return to him.

Gareth was twenty-seven and sole owner of a vast estate, but life had left him little to hope for. He'd lost his parents long ago, and his wife to childbirth when he was only twenty. He'd been a fool to marry so young, but he and Clarissa had been childhood sweethearts. After Clarissa and the babe had died, he sought ways to fill the bleak void in his heart that grew larger with each passing year. He gambled, drank—everything a man of leisure could afford—and still could not find peace. His restlessness had reared its ugly head when he had challenged Martin Banks to a duel.

Either he would lose the duel or be executed for killing Banks in an illegal duel. It should have ended tonight, but he'd been confounded by Helen. He'd been moved by her courage to take her brother's place. Like the songbird, she affected him deeply...in ways he had not begun to fully understand. He had to have her, had to hear her song in the whisper of his name, the sighs full of ecstasy, and the laugh of triumph from his own lips as he claimed her. She was a creature of sunlight, spirit, and innocence, and he craved her like he'd never craved anything in his life. He was a bastard to use her for his pleasure because her brother owed him. But damned if he didn't still desire her with a wild and unbridled hunger he hadn't felt since he'd last held his wife in his arms. He would have been lucky to recapture just one bit of that feeling again, but with Helen, it flooded through him, a tidal wave he could not stop, nor did he wish to.

When her crying stopped, and Gareth could hear no more sounds from her room, he headed toward his own bedchamber. Mary appeared at his side. She was a wizened woman in her early fifties and had been with Gareth's family since Gareth's mother was a bride.

"Might I have a word, Master Gareth?" she asked gravely, her voice low and disapproving. While Gareth had no interest in being lectured like a naughty schoolboy, he did not dare refuse her the right to chastise him for his wrongdoing. He had practically abducted the poor girl, after all.

"Yes Mary," he leaned heavily against the frame of the doorway to his own chambers.

"I know it has been awhile since you've had a woman in this house. Might I advise sending to Bath for gowns that suit her? It would not be proper for her to wear Mrs. Fairfax's clothes."

This remark astounded him. Did Mary think he'd brought home a bit of muslin? Not a woman worthy of compassion? He caught himself suddenly astonished that he'd wished to defend Helen's character. How had she wormed her way into his heart so quickly?

"I'm afraid I don't take your meaning," he growled at Mary, daring her to make another remark against Helen. After everything that had happened to her—most of it his fault—he felt protective of her.

Mary blinked, then narrowed her eyes with annoyance. "I meant no offense to the young lady by saying she was not good enough to wear Mrs. Fairfax's clothes, sir...rather I meant that she is a great deal taller than Lady Clarissa was, and her fairer hair and skin require a much different color in gowns, not to mention fashion has changed in the last seven years. If you would permit me, I will send for a better wardrobe for her tomorrow morning." Mary lifted her chin, crossing her arms with an annoyed expression, as if expecting him to growl again.

Gareth relaxed considerably. "Yes, do what you see fit. I care not for fashion, but if it would make her happy..." He trailed off, surprised that he was thinking of what would please Helen when at first she'd only been an object brought here to please him. It seemed he'd been quite moved by her tears.

"Do you wish for me to take a look at your injury?" Mary's eyes dropped to his bloodied arm.

He gave a short jerk of his head. "'Tis only a scratch. Miss Banks took it upon herself to shoot me."

"Shoot you?" His housekeeper's voice rose an octave. "And

what, pray tell, were you doing to her that warranted such a reaction?"

He flashed her a weary, yet still charming grin. "Well, that's the thing. I challenged her brother to a duel, and she showed up dressed like him and took his place. She shot me, accidentally, I think, before I realized she wasn't a man."

"Well, if you think you're well enough..." She was still eyeing the wound with worry. "I think I'll send for the doctor tomorrow and have him look it over in any case. Goodnight, sir." Mary curtsied, the corners of her mouth twitching so slightly he wondered if he'd imagined it before she left him to his thoughts and he readied for bed.

He stripped off his bloodied shirt and poured some water into his basin. The wound was superficial. The bullet had barely grazed him. He chuckled softly as he recalled Helen's wide, horrified eyes as she ran to help him in the field. Her first time to fire a pistol and she had managed to graze him—not bad for a woman.

And what a woman she was. She was truly beautiful with her soft, yielding lips of a green girl, the swell of perfect breasts, and the curve of a slender waist out to her wider hips. Just made for his hands.

God...it has been too long since I've had a woman. Gareth almost moaned. Among the many vices he'd acquired since his wife's death, seduction of other women hadn't been one of them. He hadn't the will or desire to bed any woman he'd come across in the last seven years. Yet, the mere thought of Helen beneath him in his bed, golden waves of hair rippling out around her in rays of condensed sunlight, made him shake with desire. What pleasure he would have when he took her that first time. Her sheath would squeeze him tight as a fist, and he knew the pleasure would be beyond compare. It had taken every bit of restraint he possessed to do no more than bring her to climax with his hand. His cock tightened in his breeches, shoving hard against the buttons.

He would have to control himself. She was a virgin. He had no doubt of that, not after he'd kissed her in the drawing room. She had been dewy-eyed with the innocent desire of an untouched maiden, yet she'd responded with a sensual hunger that marked her for a future as a great lover to a lucky man. She would learn just how good it felt to have him deep inside her while his lips drank from the sweetness of her mouth. Perhaps, he might at last find the pleasure he sought, after having had it torn from him seven years ago.

Gareth finished cleaning his shoulder and dressed the wound with a light bandage. As he settled into his own bed, he expected to dream of Helen and how he would seduce her come morning.

Instead, his dreams were haunted by the caged thrush and its fight for freedom, trilling a sad song into the murky depths of his unconsciousness.

HELEN WOKE WELL RESTED AND REFRESHED, SO MUCH SO THAT she almost forgot the troubles from earlier that morning. But the moment her eyes took in the foreign bed lit by sunlight, she remembered where she was. Helen slid out from under the covers to stand, the wood floor cool beneath her bare feet. She washed her face in the water basin and went to the armoire to see what clothes she might find. As much as she had enjoyed the freedom of her brother's attire, it was not wise to put it on again.

She needed a clear mind to deal with Gareth. She faced this truth with the light of day heavy upon her. The bargain they'd struck early in the morning had to be undone. Surely he would realize that after his temper had cooled and he'd rested. There was no need to keep her here, not when he could have his pick of the ladies of Bath.

Pressing her fingers to her lips, she could swear she still felt his kiss. Her memories of the early morning were merely exaggerated dreams. What they'd done together, the way they'd embraced, touched...it hadn't been that deliciously wonderful had it? Yes, that was a dream, no doubt spurred on by her anxiety of the situation.

The only thing left for her to do was decide how to tell Gareth she meant to break the bargain they'd struck and convince him to let her return home. Excuses would have to be made in order to hide where she'd been. Perhaps she could say she was ill and stayed at a friend's house... But what friend did she have who would reinforce the lie? It was unlikely that would happen, and that wasn't her only problem. She would have to find a reputable means of repaying Martin's debts. In order to do that, she must return to Bath immediately, and she would not do it garbed in men's clothing. Her family's name was already shamed enough by Martin's gambling debts, she could not add to it.

The armoire was full of dresses, each lovely yet simple. The cuts and styles were a few years out of date, but the stitching and fabrics were far finer than she was used to. She chose a pale cerulean gown that had van-dyked sleeves and a modest neckline. It was too short in the skirts, but Helen didn't mind. She dressed in a light white chemise, petticoats, and stays and was in the act of donning the gown when her door was unlocked and Mary entered.

"Good morning, Miss Banks. I trust you slept well?" Mary came over to help her dress.

"I did, thank you," she replied shyly. She'd had to let her ladies' maid, Olivia, go a few months ago. Servants were far too costly to maintain without money when she and her brother could barely afford to eat. Mary made quick work of letting out the hem of the dress with a small pair of sewing scissors.

"The master has permitted me to send for gowns more suitable to your height and coloring. They'll be here later today," Mary said as she gestured for Helen to sit in front of the vanity table.

"I do not wish to inconvenience him," Helen said, distressed to hear that this might in some way further the great debt between them. Mary shushed her as she brushed Helen's hair and began to style it.

Mary seemed able to read her thoughts. "It was at my request. He thinks little of the expense, and it is no inconvenience."

Can I allow him to do this for me? The thought of lovely gowns, a whole pile of them just for her...it was almost too much. And she hated herself for wanting them, even just to look at.

"There now, a vision of loveliness. Do not let the master muss it up," she warned with a secretive smile. Helen blushed, her skin radiating with the implications of Mary's warning.

When Helen turned and stared at herself in the mirror, she marveled at the style the housekeeper had chosen. Mary had pulled her locks back loosely into a rippling coil much in the Grecian style. Several loose curls fell against the back of her neck, and a matching cerulean ribbon threaded about her hair held it all in place.

"I did not think anyone save the master woke at such an early hour. The breakfast will not be ready for another hour. Perhaps you would care to see the gardens?" Mary suggested as she ushered Helen out of the bedchamber.

"I'm sure the gardens will be lovely," she said, but when her stomach rumbled, she blushed in shame.

"Oh dear, come to the kitchens with me and I'll see you get something into that belly of yours before you go out." The house-keeper tugged one of her curls playfully, the gesture so warm and fond that Helen blinked back tears. Her mother used to do that—tug a curl and kiss her cheek.

Helen started to protest, but the hunger pains only grew and she didn't see a point in fighting. Mary ushered her out of the bedchamber and led her towards the kitchens.

Gareth's house, so haunting and dark at night, was a different creature altogether in the light of day. Sun broke through the many windows, lighting up paintings of pastoral scenes and gardens which decorated the walls. It was as though the house's inhabitants had wanted to feel they were forever in the gardens, even while inside the walls. And yet, despite its beauty, something felt hollow here. Helen thought of when she'd been a child and she'd found an abandoned nest in the late fall. This house had that same feel...as though it, too, had lost those who'd once dwelt within its walls.

"Mary, has this house always been so lonely?" She knew it was impertinent to ask, but her curiosity demanded an answer.

"The master lost his wife and child seven years ago. He was only a lad then, barely twenty. The house has been quiet since my lady's passing." Mary sighed heavily as though it pained her to speak of the loss.

"Mr. Fairfax is only twenty-seven?" She was astounded by this. He did not look old, but his voice, his gaze, his physical presence seemed to her to be so worldly, so experienced. To think, he was only six years her senior. Helen repressed the sudden flare of irritation at his treating her as though she were a mere babe at times. Then her irritation faded in the wake of a tremor at how he'd kissed her in her chamber. Maybe he didn't think of her as being so young after all.

The kitchens were bustling with busy servants, and Helen lingered in the doorway, afraid to intrude. Mary gathered a couple of cookies and ushered her back into the hallway. Helen took the treats and nibbled on them as she followed the housekeeper to a door at the rear of the house.

"Ah, here we are. The gardens are just beyond. Should you fancy a longer walk, there is a nice meadow outside. But do not stray far. It is easy to get lost. We are quite far from any village." Mary shoved her gently out the door.

The second Mary was gone, Helen started walking, keeping her pace slow as she finished the last of the cookies and put a hand to her stomach, relishing the satisfied feeling. She had the strangest urge to run, to escape. Knowing Gareth was somewhere close made her feel...vulnerable, exposed. Early that morning, she'd been certain she could handle him and be happy to share his bed. But sleeping had returned her good sense. She wasn't prepared for a joining with a man, especially not one like Gareth. He'd barge into her heart, steal it away, and leave her body restless for him and his kisses for the rest of her life. A woman simply could not afford that sort of problem, not when she'd likely have to beg on the streets to save what remained of her family.

She paused to cup flowers in her hands and breathe their scent in. But she never forgot for a moment that she should be working up the courage to speak to Gareth and break off their agreement.

He must be up and about somewhere on the estate, if Mary's words were any evidence. Helen still felt unprepared to see him again. It would be too easy to get lost in the memory of his mouth on hers, his hand stroking between her thighs in that dark, hot place. As though she'd summoned her own demon of passion, the spot between her legs throbbed steadily—insistently—for Gareth's expert touch.

She finally located the garden's exit, deciding it might be better to get further away from the house for a while and hoping the fresh air would clear her head.

The exit was a stone archway with a wooden door covered in climbing ivy. Helen dug around the slick ivy leaves to find the handle and cracked the door open. Beyond it, she found a sprawling scene of beautiful land, trees dotting the edges of the rolling meadows, and azure skies stretching to the heavens themselves. As she passed through the archway, she had the strangest sense that she was free of Gareth and the binding of their devil's bargain. Behind her was the house and his control, ahead of her was only open land. She could go where she wished...

I'm a fool to think he won't come after me. He would find her, she had no doubt, but the illusion of freedom was something she wouldn't take for granted, even for so short a time.

Fluffy white shapes dotted a distant sloping hill. *They must be sheep.* Her heart skipped a beat at the beauty. It reminded her so much of her childhood home, a small cottage, far away from here, which had abutted an estate as grand as this. Surely she had taken a wrong turn outside the garden gate. This had to be paradise, not Gareth's lands.

Damn Martin and his gambling. If only he'd controlled himself. I'd never have ended up here, seen this place, or kissed Gareth.

Helen was halfway through the meadow when it occurred to her that she ought to seek shelter in the trees where he could not see her, if she wished to have her moment alone to clear her head. Given that Gareth had locked her in her room last night, he might think she intended to escape if he saw her in the meadow.

She changed direction, walking parallel to the house as she headed toward the nearest copse of trees. She turned back once more, pausing to see the house one last time before she left. The soft snap of twigs and the brush of cloth made her spin back around. Gareth was lounging against a tree six feet away from her.

"Taking a walk, Helen?" The way he caressed her name made her shiver. He was dressed in tan breeches and a waistcoat of dark navy blue, so at odds with the greens and umber browns of the woods behind him.

"Good Morning, Mr. Fairfax." She gave a nod of greeting but looked away from his openly admiring gaze. It was all too familiar to the way he'd looked upon her last night when he'd pinned her against the bedpost and... Heat infused her cheeks and flashed beneath the surface of her skin.

He shifted away from the tree he'd been leaning against. "Please, call me Gareth. You are looking well. Blushing suits you."

"Er... Thank you." She wasn't sure if she ought to have thanked him for such a comment, but she did it anyway, trying to maintain a pretense of calm. Her eyes scanned the area on either side of him, trying to determine the best route to get around him. He was blocking her best path.

"I should like to continue my walk...Gareth. Would you let me pass?" She finally summoned the courage to look him in the eye.

It was a mistake.

His eyes burned her, invisible flames flicking over her skin, heating her from the inside out. The throbbing started between her thighs again and she clenched them together, but the pressure only made the throbbing worse.

"And let you run off and get lost? My darling Helen, I'd much rather you stay here so I don't have to find you later." The grin of devilish delight playing with his lips was far too charming and far too dangerous. He took a step closer.

Helen's heartbeat increased. If she ran now, would he dare to grab her? It would be so uncivilized. Yet there was something distinctly *uncivilized* about him. The predatory way he stalked her and the primal way he'd taken control of her body earlier that morning in her chamber set her ablaze inside. Helen darted to the left, choosing the opening between Gareth and the tree. He lunged, catching her easily by wrapping one arm around her waist. She was too startled to scream as he backed her up against the rough bark. Her hands clenched at his chest, catching the smooth fabric of his waistcoat. He gripped her waist, holding her firm and preventing her from escaping him.

"Helen ..." he whispered, his voice strangely soothing, calming. "I'm not going to hurt you. I made a promise, and I keep my promises." A ghost of a smile hovered at his mouth. "But I am going to kiss you."

Her traitorous body relaxed in his hold. Her eyes drifted shut, her head tilting upward for his kiss. But his lips never touched hers. Instead they trailed softly from her neck down to the swell of her breasts. Her breathing deepened, her chest rising to meet his exploring mouth. With each inhalation, she struggled to stay above the drowning sense of dizziness that his touch roused in her. He cupped one of the tender mounds, his thumb circling her hardened nipple through the fabric of her gown. He pinched the bud and Helen forgot breathing all together. His eyes were lowered, studying her reaction—the way her skin flushed as he continued to tease and torture the sensitive peak. Helen was fascinated by his intense expression, the way his lips were slightly parted, his breath rougher, his eyes half-lidded but their gleam sharp. When his fingers pinched her nipple again, she gasped, drawing his focus back up to her face.

"You are so responsive, so alive," he murmured, his thumb caressing her cheek. "You don't even know what that does to me, do you?"

Helen swallowed, her mouth dry and incapable of forming words.

Gareth's hands wound around her waist, pulling her away from the tree and toward the edge of the meadow.

"Sit," he urged gently.

Still entranced by the way he kept her spellbound with his soft, arousing words and touches, she allowed him to help her down onto the ground. He pressed her shoulders, urging her to lie back. The grass bent beneath her when he cradled one arm behind her head as a firm pillow.

"What are we doing?" she whispered, studying his face, the sunlight haloing him as he leaned over her.

"Getting acquainted," he replied, as though what they were doing was the most normal thing in all the world.

"Wouldn't that entail you courting me by bringing me flowers and sitting in the parlor under the watchful eyes of a chaperone?" She was half joking, trying to fight off the tingle of nervousness that made its way through her body with small tremors.

His rich laugh made her smile. He could be teasing and playful then. Knowing that eased more of the tension inside her and she relaxed.

"Do you want flowers? I can promise you a field of wildflowers, a garden, even a hothouse. Whatever you desire, it is yours. But no chaperones and no parlors. I want you, want to know your body and the way it responds to mine." His earnestness surprised her. He seemed as baffled by his answering hunger for her.

She squirmed, trying to stop his hand from pushing up her skirts, but he gently pushed her hand away. Helen's eyes widened as his other hand slid beneath her gown and up her left thigh. The dress's fabric rose obligingly at his hand's command, taking her petticoats with it. Helen's mouth parted as she gasped in shock and her sudden fear of vulnerability. She was terrified of his hand on her bare thigh and even more scared by how she wanted him to keep moving his palm higher even though she guessed where it would lead. Did all women feel this way when first touched by a man, torn between desperation to escape and the need for more?

Gareth's face blocked out the bright sky. Would he give her pleasure like last night?

"Do not fear me, Helen." It almost sounded like a plea.

But if Helen knew anything about a man like Gareth Fairfax, she knew he was not the sort of man to beg. Rather, the hunger that flamed behind his dark brown eyes explained everything. He needed her body, needed to have her accept whatever it was he wished to do. What could a woman say to that? *Yes, take me, take all of me?* She wasn't nearly ready for that sort of surrender to him. The thought was erased as Gareth's head descended toward hers.

His lips found hers. She was lost to the pleasure of his tongue dancing with hers but still aware of his hand as it parted her legs and slid through the slit in her drawers. That first brush of his fingertips on her hot flesh burned them both, her with a hiss and him with a groan. Helen shifted restlessly as wetness pooled between her thighs. He moved deeper, finding the swollen flesh tender and yearning. He stroked her once, twice, opening her further to him. She shivered in pleasure as he continued. Her legs twisted and shifted as she adjusted to the strange sensation of his invading touch. It was as though he was caressing the innermost part of her. Each slow thrust of his fingers was a delicious teasing. Gareth's mouth left hers again to lay kisses along the lines of her collarbone and down to the heavy swell of her breasts.

A pain grew deep within her, a hunger between her legs, the same desire that she'd felt this morning in her room. She clutched Gareth's shoulders. As though he understood her body's needs, his fingers sunk deeper into her, and she let out a small cry of pleasure mingled with fear. Pinpricks of tiny explosions burst forth, sending tremors outward along her limbs. She clung to him, her violent quaking subsiding against the strength of his embrace.

He withdrew his hand, pulling her petticoats and gown back down over her hips and legs. He kissed her again, the meeting of mouths softer than before, as though he sought to maintain the intimacy of that moment—their closeness and the isolation they found together in the meadow. He held her against him and Helen breathed in his scent. Sandalwood, leather, and something uniquely belonging to him, intoxicating as an opiate. The breeze moved the grass around them like waves of an emerald sea. For a brief moment, Helen thought they were the only two people in this paradise, and that no world existed outside.

"Do I still frighten you?" Gareth asked, his tone teasing as he stroked her cheek.

Helen, spellbound by the sensations he'd created in her moments ago, was speechless for a second. She leaned into his caress, unable to deny herself the pleasure of his touch. She could not escape him, and she was beginning to want to stay. But a part of her still feared him, the way he made her want things she knew she could never have, like happiness with a man like him. She remembered the fire in his eyes as he demanded the debt be paid. He would claim it—claim her—and that did frighten her. What would happen when he was done and she'd been foolish enough to let herself fall for him?

"I believe you will always frighten me," she admitted. But it was a different sort of fear, not one of harm to the body, but devastation to the heart.

His laugh was low and rough. "You present me with a challenge then. I shall spend our time together wooing you into trusting me." He fingered one of her loosened curls, wearing a boyish smile. "I rather like you, Helen."

She bit her lip, the words *I rather like you, too* hung on the tip of her tongue, unspoken.

He got to his feet, brushing grass off his breeches. "Should we return to the house and see if Mary has breakfast ready?"

She wobbled for a few seconds as he pulled her to her feet. Her legs trembled, still reverberating with the memory of what he'd done to her and how her body had reacted. Echoes of pleasure still worked their way through her in little flushes and the twitching of her inner muscles. He held out an arm, which she leaned on, grateful for the support.

The house was abuzz with the flutter of servants when they

returned. Maids were dusting shelves and polishing candlesticks. Footmen were stretching their legs by running errands at Mary's bidding. She stood in the main hall, issuing orders better than a British General. Gareth nodded in greeting as they passed her on their way to the dining room. She smiled, brief but warm, before dashing off to chastise a clumsy footman who'd tripped on the edge of a carpet and spilled the basin of water he'd been carrying.

The table was decorated with plates of fruit, eggs, kippers, and various jams for spreading on a stack of warm toast. Helen's stomach growled at the sight of food. Even though she'd stuffed herself on cookies an hour ago, the sight of these new dishes renewed her hunger. Over the last few months, she had survived on small portions of bread and water, just to be able to get by. She'd taken to giving her brother the larger share of whatever meals they could afford. Gareth pulled out a chair for her next to his own seat at the head of the table. Helen reached for the nearest piece of toast but froze, remembering her manners. Gareth had not yet made a move towards the food. His eyes were scanning a stack of letters brought in by a servant. He glanced up, noticing her stillness.

"Do not wait for me. Please eat." He smiled warmly at her. She had to stop herself before she smiled back. He was a different person from early this morning. Then, he'd been a haunted, troubled man, burdened by anger and frustration. Now he seemed... kind. Even in the meadow, his touch had been soft, insistent, too, but not brutal...not like what she'd expected.

Helen filled a plate with a balance of fruits, eggs, and toast, enjoying the variety. There was a flare of excitement in her at being able to eat as much as she wanted. Their fortune had been so slight that meals had been meager of late, and she'd been forced to convince Martin that she wasn't nearly as hungry as he was so that he might have a fuller belly. For the first time since her father died, she was able to worry only about herself, about what she needed. Her stomach grumbled again, and Helen eyed the stack of toast thoughtfully before quickly snatching another piece and adding it to her plate.

This strange sense of comfort and ease made her less and less willing to fight against Gareth and his desires. If she liked what happened in the meadow, she would probably like other things he might do to her. Well, if she was being truly honest, she hadn't just liked it. She'd reveled in it. It might be worth it—his physical pleasure traded for food and clothing. A cold thought struck her. Was she no better than the type of women she'd feared she would become? Surely not. Gareth didn't treat her like she was that sort of woman, but still... Helen shook her head slightly to rid herself of that unpleasant thought and turned her attention back to the food.

Gareth read his letters as he ate, seemingly oblivious to her study of him. She thought perhaps her mind had exaggerated the marble carved features of perfection on his face, but they were just as she had remembered. The sunlight played with his hair, revealing a hint of chocolate brown amidst the rich russet. His hands were large and strong, the fingers deftly breaking the seals of his letters. Those were the same hands that had brought unspeakable pleasure to her only a short while ago. A delicious little shiver ran through her at the memory.

When Gareth finished his breakfast, he bid her a good day with a genteel bow, lifting her hand to press his lips on the inside of her wrist. Her pulse jumped at the intimate contact.

She was fascinated by him, like a helpless minnow spying its first shiny lure in the stream. Helen wanted to follow him, to see where he would go and what he would do. Would he want to kiss her or pleasure her again? Gareth was halfway out the door when he paused and Helen bumped into his back. He looked over his shoulder at her as though surprised to find her so close.

"You mean to follow me, Helen? I do not expect you to. You are free to go about the house and gardens as you wish."

Helen frowned. Was he dismissing her? Did he mean to leave her alone while he went about his day? The thought saddened her.

Perhaps she was not a good companion and he would soon tire of her. As a twin, she craved companionship, and didn't like too much time alone. She didn't need to be speaking to someone every minute of the day, but she liked another person in her presence. Perhaps Gareth was the opposite and did not wish to have her around.

Her unhappy silence affected him enough that he reached out for her arm and tilted his head to indicate she should accompany him.

"Come along then. I'm off to the stables. It is a fine day for riding."

"You have horses?" She was all smiles again, memories of her youth flooding through her. They'd once owned a pair of stout draft horses, and she and Martin used to ride them in the summer.

"Of course I have horses, my darling. How do you think my coach brought you here?"

He was teasing her, she could see it in his eyes. She liked it when he was playful. He must feel something for her, however small, if he joked with her. One of Martin's boyhood friends used to tug her hair, and her mother said that men often treated the women they liked in such a fashion.

"Do you know how to ride?"

"I do, but not sidesaddle, I'm afraid," she admitted. Her father hadn't bothered with teaching her the niceties expected of gentle bred ladies, at least when it came to riding. Since her mother died when she was a child, she'd been without the feminine guidance that would have taught her such things.

"That is well, for I got rid of the only sidesaddle I had years ago."

"Because your wife passed away?" She regretted the words the moment they came out. "I'm sorry. I did not mean to..." she was flustered, her face warm with embarrassment.

"Do not worry. I have mourned Clarissa, my wife, and am at peace with her death. You may speak about her if you wish. It will not cause me pain, I assure you." Despite the polite smile that curved his lips, there was a guarded wariness in his face that said there was still a twist in his heart at the mention of his late wife.

"You loved her very much." Helen saw it in his eyes, the way the sadness there formed dark shadows. Losing someone you loved often left a stain upon the soul.

"She was my friend. Not many men are fortunate enough to have wives who lay claim to their hearts and their minds, not just as lovers but also as friends. It's a loss not easy to recover from. I mourn the way we used to talk late into the night and ride together on lazy afternoons." He gave a little shake of his head, as though to dispel the creeping melancholy. "We were happy when many around us were not so fortunate. I'll likely never know that sense of joy again."

Helen bit her bottom lip, pain clamping its vice-like claws on her own heart, threatening to rip it asunder. Gareth was a wounded man still, no matter that he believed he'd moved on. Everything about him was becoming clearer, he was desperate to feel, to live again, and using her, even as a temporary companion, must be one way in which he was trying to find solace. She did not feel pity, but rather it filled her with compassion.

With false cheeriness, he gestured to the stairs. "Would you like to go and change into a riding habit?"

"Yes. I shall only be a moment," she promised.

Once Helen was properly attired for riding, they left the house and approached the building next to it. It was a small but well-kept stable with four stalls for the four horses he owned. They were all matching bays with tall heads and long, lean legs, nothing like the draft horses she'd ridden as a child.

Even though she didn't want to cause him distress, she still wanted to get to know him. If she were to stay here with him, she'd have to understand him better. "If you no longer miss your wife, why haven't you remarried?"

How could this man, so blessed in looks and fortune, not find another wife, one who would delight in pleasing him? Gareth smiled, though it was little and pained. His eyes moved from the horse to her. She read the truth there. Clarissa couldn't be replaced and he hadn't wanted to try.

"I got used to Clarissa's absence after a few years, but I've become restless. Nothing eases me anymore, nothing gives me peace." He spoke softly, more to himself as though the revelation was one he'd never dared to voice aloud. His confession was like opening a book, the pages revealing a glimpse of his secrets. She craved to read more of his soul, to come to know him the way he knew only himself.

Helen wished to comfort him, so she put a hand on his arm. "Try to love again. Love settle's a person's heart."

He shook his head. "No. Love destroys. It rips you clean in two and devastates you. I would never go looking for that again."

GARETH LOOKED AT HER, HER BLUE EYES GAZING AT HIM IN pity. Did she not know what she was asking of him? Love was hard to find, hard to earn, and hard to keep. He reached up to tug one of her curls playfully, wanting to rid his mind of the thoughts she'd put there. His actions made her wrinkle her nose in disapproval. The urge to hold her was too strong to resist. He tugged her into his arms, relishing the feel of her body flush against his.

She was growing ever more receptive to his kisses. He let her mouth guide his, let her explore his chest, his arms, his back before she locked her hands around his neck. Her fingertips brushed the back of his neck and stroked his hair. He loved how quickly she opened up to him, how she let him instruct her in the ways of seduction.

The feeling of her touch on his skin made him shiver. She was a quick learner. Gareth wanted to part her legs again, like he'd done in the meadow, but the stables were no place for such an activity. Instead he teased her breasts through the fabric of her gown until he felt her grow breathless. He hardened, his groin aching with need, but he could not take her, not until she asked for him. He could have kissed and touched her for hours.

"My apologies, sir!" A groom, who'd walked into the stables, apologized profusely as he scrambled away, overturning a bucket of feed in his haste to depart.

Helen stifled an embarrassed giggle and buried her face in his chest as though to hide herself from the world. Gareth found himself laughing, too. It was a loud, rich laugh, one he hadn't made in years. What was she doing to him? In a mere matter of a day, she had turned his world upside down. She was open and honest about herself and her life. And brave. He couldn't forget that, either, the way she'd risked her life to save her brother's knowing she would die. What woman of his acquaintance would have dared to risk her life? None that he knew. Helen was different. She was real and beautiful and so full of life. Each time he looked at her, something inside him seemed to shake off a century's worth of dust and awaken. Being around her made him feel alive.

"Let's get the horses ready. We should get a ride in while the day is young." Gareth reluctantly pried her away from his chest and set about saddling the horses.

They rode at a nice canter for nearly an hour, over the meadow, down the hill, and through the neighboring lands. Gareth chuckled as Helen rode her mare through a flock of panicked sheep. They both nearly fell out of their saddles with laughter as they watched the wooly creatures bolt in all directions to avoid being trampled by her horse. The sheep gathered rebelliously into a flock several yards away, bleating melodramatically at having been attacked.

"Heavens! That was quite a ride," Helen said as she watched the sheep shifting restlessly as her horse stomped and huffed.

"I daresay, the farmer, Mr. Pennysworth, won't be pleased to find we've been scaring his beasts. Come, let's away, Helen," He chuckled and lightly tugged the reins of his horse, guiding it to turn around.

Gareth watched Helen the entire time they were out riding. He could not keep his eyes off the halo of her golden hair or the mischievous grin as she drove towards the sheep. Her little laugh was music to him, music he'd been missing for years.

Sing my little thrush, please sing to me. She was beautiful, she was perfect, and he would have to let her go. That brother of hers would eventually show up, and Gareth would have to deal with him when the time came. Damned if he knew what to do with Martin Banks. The fool might still insist on the duel, now over Helen's honor. What a mess he was in. His eyes strayed to Helen, and her easy smile made all of the problems with his choice to have her fade. She was worth the trouble. He knew he could not keep her for long. Ambrose's words came back to him. He was ruining her for her brother's debts. Debts she shouldn't have to pay, and he'd destroyed all chances of her making a good match. On the field after the duel that hadn't mattered to him, in fact he'd relished the thought of hurting Banks by saddling him with a sister who would never make a match. But now...now he saw he was only hurting Helen, a brave, innocent woman who didn't deserve any of this. Yet there was no way to undo the damage he'd done.

Marriage was out of the question. He had nothing to offer her besides his name and his body, and he knew only too well that a woman like Helen would need his heart to survive a marriage. For him, it was seduction, plain and simple. He had no right to anything else. He'd lost his right to love a long time ago. God would not give him a second chance, not after blessing him with Clarissa. That sort of love, he was sure, came only once. He had his turn and lost. Helen was nothing more than a cruel reminder of what he could never have.

THE DUELIST'S SEDUCTION

CHAPTER 3

Helen spent the remainder of the day exploring the house, reading in the expansive library, and being spoiled by the numerous cooks in the kitchen, who were more than delighted to let her taste pies, pastries, and other dishes they were preparing. Gareth had to leave on a business related matter but had assured her he would return in time for dinner. Helen found the house felt empty with his departure at first, but Mary soon distracted her with activities. She was allowed to play freely on the pianoforte in the music room, she was encouraged to explore the gardens, and she was positively forced to try on gown after gown once they arrived late in the afternoon from Bath. About halfway through the day, Helen was sure this was an elaborate and wonderful dream, and that eventually, she would wake to find herself back in Bath, ever watchful of her brother and their meager finances.

Once Mary had finished fitting all of the new gowns, she left Helen to her own devices. The day was still clear and fine and the warm sun was setting in the western sky as Helen entered the gardens once more. She found a stout tree near the garden wall and decided to climb it to better see the sunset. Climbing was something more suited for a young child, not a woman of one and twenty, but she couldn't find it in herself to care. Here, she was free to do as she wished, to eat, to play, to laugh, even to climb. In this private world, she had been swept away by the sense of time-lessness. She could do whatever she wanted, and at the moment, she planned to climb a tree to get a better glimpse of the reddening skies beyond the gardens.

Returning to her chamber, she quickly donned her brother's breeches and shirt. It was the best attire for climbing. Her new white muslin gown would have been completely ruined. Helen shared her brother's athletic build and found it easy to grasp the lowest branches and hoist herself up. The bark was rough beneath her palms, but she ignored the sting of the minor scrapes on her sensitive skin. By the time she stopped ascending, she had a fair view of the sunset over the garden wall.

The sun was now a crimson apple hanging low on the horizon as though waiting to be plucked. Thick beams of gold light tickled the waving grasses of the meadow, deepening the emerald colors. It was that one hour of the day so often missed during the bustle of activity, when the world seemed frozen in that golden span of time. A hush descended over the land, bird chatter was quieter, and no breezes whipped the branches or grass. There was only a soft silence, like when a mother puts her babe to sleep in the late afternoon. The air was filled with the promise of what night might bring, yet the flurry of activity for the evening had not begun. It was a sacred time.

"How the devil did you get up there?" Gareth's voice boomed.

Helen jerked, nearly falling from the branch she balanced on. She glanced down, seeing him at the base of the tree, looking up at her. Ten feet separated her from Gareth and the ground. It was no great distance, really.

"I climbed, of course." She laughed at his look of surprise, her heart sliding down from her throat and back into her chest as she steadied herself again. "How did you find me?"

His brows drew down into a slight frown. One of the gardeners saw you come out here in your brother's clothes. He was worried you were planning to leave, so he kept track of where you went.

This time, it was she who frowned. "You've had your servants watching me?"

"Well..." He glanced away, guilty. "Not really. I merely told them you were not to leave the grounds without me. It was more the fact that you were walking around in breeches that got the man's attention, rather than my order for him to keep an eye on you," Gareth answered.

"Oh," she exhaled. It did make sense. She'd jumped to conclusions about him and had been wrong—well, not entirely—but still wrong enough to feel the uncomfortable weight of her own guilt at making such suppositions.

"Shall I call the head gardener for his ladder?"

She sighed. "No, I can get down. I just wanted to see the sunset." Her eyes once more returned to the peach colored skies aflame around the setting sun. She could have stayed there forever, watching the slowly changing colors, forgetting every worry that hung heavy on her soul.

The tree gave a little shake and branches whispered around her. She glanced back down to see Gareth climbing up toward her. He balanced himself at the fork of the large branch she was sitting on and the base of the tree. He tested the branch to see if it would hold his weight. There was a single moment, when he raised his eyes to her face, that she saw something in his expression that gave her a little shiver. Desire and contentment tinged with desperation as he gazed upon her, as though she were a great prize held high above his reach. No one had *ever* looked at her that way. She knew enough women who would have used that look to their advantage, but her first instinct was to go to him, to kiss away the sorrow in his eyes and the tightness of his mouth. Even though he'd ruined her, she couldn't resist him.

When he was satisfied the tree would hold him, he opened his arms to her. Without thinking, Helen slid over to nestle herself back against him as they watched the sunset together.

"How was your day?" His warm breath stirred the curls of hair dangling against her neck.

"Wonderful. Absolutely wonderful. It has been so long since..." She caught herself.

"So long since what?" His lips pressed lightly against her cheek. She shut her eyes, wishing she could tell him, but shame kept her quiet.

"Tell me, Helen." Her name on his lips weakened her resolve to remain silent.

Silence fell between them as she hesitated. He didn't press her to speak. He simply held onto her, as though they had countless hours to simply exist together in the same sphere, a single word unneeded. It was this sense of comfort he created that made her able to trust him with the vulnerable truth of her situation.

"It has been so long since I had a day where I could do as I wished, not have to save my food so Martin could have more, not have to mend yet another tear in my only shawl, not have to fear the whispers and societal slights against me and my brother at the assembly rooms. A day where I could be myself." She felt the tell-tale burn of a blush, but she couldn't stop it.

Gareth, whose hand had been rubbing up and down her back, stilled the movement. For a breathless moment, she feared he'd move away.

"How long has your brother been losing money at the tables?"

"For nearly three months. He only waited a month after our father died before he started frequenting the gambling hells. We started out with so little. He claimed he could win enough to keep us well situated in Bath. We had only just moved here a few weeks after Papa died. We took a pair of small rooms with a low rent, but Martin said we needed more. That's when he began haunting the card tables."

Gareth's hands rubbed her hips, the touch soothing, rather than erotic. "I take it he never listened to you when you asked him to stop."

"No. The first few times he returned with his pockets empty, I fought with him. Our rows were terrible, and we said unforgivable things to each other. After that, he started slipping out after I retired to bed each night. I knew what he was up to, of course. In the mornings, his eyes were red and his clothes rumpled as though he'd slept in them. It was so obvious, but there was little I could do to stop him." Helen's voice broke as raw, painful emotions ripped through her.

Gareth said nothing and his silence worried her. Would he cast her out? Now that he knew the truth? He caught her chin, turning her face towards his. His eyes were warm and compassionate as he breathed two words.

"My darling…" He kissed her softly, sweetly. "I'm so sorry."

It was just the sort of kiss she had thought would be her first, one full of emotion where heat was secondary. Yet there was passion behind the tenderness. She could feel it in the depth of his lips and the warmth of his arm that encircled his waist.

Gareth finally broke the kiss, but he rested his forehead against hers, keeping her close as though he didn't desire to separate himself from her. "We should get down. Mary will be angry if we are late for dinner."

He climbed down first and held out his arms for her to jump. The invitation to give herself to him was beyond compelling. She resisted, climbing down the last few branches on her own until she saw the hurt in his eyes. Hesitating, she studied his face. His expression was so different than before. Pleading glimmered in his eyes, and she let herself surrender to him, allowing him to help her down the last branch to the ground.

Mary kidnapped Helen the moment they were both inside.

"Look at the state of the pair of you! Covered in leaves and heaven knows what else," she chastised, but Helen thought she saw a glimmer of a smile on Mary's lips.

"We've been climbing trees." Gareth flashed Helen a conspiratorial grin.

"I can *see* that, sir." Mary retorted. She plucked Helen's arm off his and took her to her bedchamber, muttering under her breath about trees "being a gardener's concern". Helen bit her tongue to stop from laughing.

"Now, let's get you cleaned up and into a proper evening gown."

Mary helped her wash up and change. Helen wore a fine burgundy evening gown with short sleeves. It had a very low neckline, which Helen kept tugging up until Mary caught her.

"Let the gown be, my dear. You have a fine figure, show it to your advantage."

"But it's dreadfully low," Helen whispered in a scandalized tone. Mary raised a wicked eyebrow.

"Yes it is."

Helen's cheeks heated but she realized it wouldn't matter. At this rate, she'd likely not be wearing the gown past dessert. She hadn't forgotten the incident in the meadow earlier that day and the promise that had lingered in Gareth's eyes. Tonight he would seduce her, fully and completely. It was inevitable and she saw little point in fighting it, especially when she knew she wanted it just as badly as he did. She was quickly becoming addicted to the ecstasy of his touch.

Mary handed Helen a gold shawl that matched her fair hair and propelled the girl into the hall. Mary watched her go on to the dining room alone. She knew Helen was an innocent young lady, and soon her master would pluck the ripe fruit that the child was unknowingly offering, but she did not pass judgment. She had known her master since he was a babe in the cradle, and he had a kind heart and a gentle soul.

These past few years, he'd fallen from a good path. But from the moment that Helen passed through the doorway, he'd been changing. Mary was not a gambling woman, but she would wager that before all this was over, her master would do right by the girl. It was clear he was exceedingly fond of her, and she was already twining him about her finger without even realizing it. Gareth

Fairfax just might be falling in love again. Perhaps there would be another wedding and another baby to fill the house. Mary let out a wistful sigh, smoothed her skirts, and headed in the direction of the kitchens.

THE DINING ROOM GLOWED BENEATH THE EVENING SUN, WHICH gilded everything in its path. The effect was like something from a fairy tale dream. Helen couldn't believe how beautiful the light was as it illuminated the table and the feast which had been laid out before her. The abundance of food was startling. She hadn't seen so much since...well, ever. After months of watching her finances, to see such luxury, the food too much for two people, her smile faltered.

"Surely we don't need this much..." she briefly closed her eyes before opening them. "I didn't speak to you this afternoon about my situation in order to provoke such lavish treatment."

He eyed her seriously. "Nothing here is wasted, I assure you. Now, come and sit by me."

Gareth gave her a small smile when she crossed the room. The warmth of his hands seeped into her bare skin when they brushed her shoulders as he seated her. Despite her worry about his subdued manner, she managed to eat the delicious dish of duck she'd been served. She sipped her wine, knowing that too much of it gave her dreadful headaches in the morning, but she felt the fortification of a little bit of spirits might help her relax tonight.

To her delight, the dessert served was raspberries. She speared one with her fork, but as she raised it up, she noticed Gareth watching her with heavy lidded eyes. He was lounging back in his chair, one hand lazily holding his glass of wine, the other stroking circles on the crimson tablecloth. Like a lazy lion, he seemed content to watch his prey flounder and panic, wondering how he would strike. She slowly slipped the raspberry into her mouth, swallowing hard as she forgot to chew.

"There are better ways to eat those." His voice was smooth as velvet and dark as night. It cast a spell on her, slowly drowning her in the thick sensuality of the look that accompanied his words. The world around them seemed to darken and then fade, leaving them alone in the decadent dining room. She was all too aware his intentions had nothing to do with the proper consumption of raspberries. It was a game, and she wanted to play.

Helen slowly lowered her fork as he leaned forward in his chair to pluck a raspberry from his plate and slip it into his mouth. She watched his lips consume the berry and a swell of heat rose below her waist. She'd had those lips on her skin before and couldn't help but wonder what they'd feel like on other parts of her skin. She flushed with desire at the images even her innocent mind seemed to conjure. His mouth upon her breast, teeth scraping over a sensitive peak while his fingers played between her legs...

"Here let me..." he said, taking another raspberry and holding it out to her. She leaned forward, her lips parting to take the fruit from his fingers. The pads of his fingertips lingered at her mouth for a long moment before she moved back. Helen took another berry and held it out to him, eager to return the intimate gesture.

Gareth's lips took the fruit, but he caught her hand before it could retreat. He sucked the raspberry juice from her fingertips. The feel of his tongue on her fingers drew a soft sigh of pleasure from her as her body flamed to life. He continued to hold her wrist as he sucked each of her fingers, one at time, into his mouth. The look of satisfaction and hunger mixing on his face only made her hotter. It was as though he loved the taste of the berry juices on her skin and nothing was more satisfying than licking it from her flesh.

"Come closer to me."

Helen slid her chair over to his and he leaned into her, offering another raspberry. Only this time, as she swallowed it, he ducked his head and licked a wicked line up her neck and nibbled her ear. He leaned deeper into her, curling one arm around her waist as he embraced her. The combined sensations of swallowing sweetness and the feel of his hot tongue dancing up her throat lit a fire between her legs. A heavy, sharp ache slashed between her thighs, shooting upward. The sensation was almost painful and she couldn't bear it another second. Instinctively, she tried to pull away, to restore some control to herself, but his grasp on her waist wouldn't let her move. Gareth offered another berry. She took it almost greedily, and again he laved her throat, this time nipping her below her ear. A stinging shiver shot straight down her spine like she'd been struck by lightning. The hairs on the back of her neck and arms rose, and she trembled with the force of her heightened arousal. Helen couldn't breathe. Wetness pooled between her legs, and she started to shake. If he did that again, she'd lose her mind and her body.

Gareth released her hand and stood up.

"Should we retire to the drawing room?"

Helen managed a nod and took his offered arm. There were no servants in the halls as they walked, but someone had come in and lit a fire in the fireplace. There were two chairs and a loveseat. Helen watched Gareth for a clue as to where she should sit. He sat down on the loveseat, removing his black waistcoat. His white shirt molded to his muscles as he moved. She watched, desperate to see the skin beneath the shirt and feel the muscles move beneath her palms. What would it be like to put her hands to his flesh? To touch the source of such pleasure, such erotic sin, that she could scarcely breathe or think?

Gareth caught her staring and put his hand on the empty part of the seat next to him, patting it once. His silent command was clear. Helen knew she should have chosen the nearest chair. But damn the man, she wanted to be near him, to touch him, to let him touch her. She was quite close to begging him to make love to her. The ache was stronger every minute she spent in his presence.

Helen sat down on the edge of the loveseat, her hands clinging to her shawl as though it would give her strength. As though sensing her use of the fabric as a shield, Gareth reached out to her shoulder, coiling his fingers into the silk shawl. He slowly pulled it away from her, and she felt every inch of the cloth as it slid over the bare skin of her upper back. He dropped the shawl to the floor, out of reach, and then slid a few inches closer, gazing deeply into her eyes.

"Ask me..." he breathed.

One of his hands drifted down her back while the other hand alighted upon her knee, sliding slowly up her leg. Gareth's brown eyes were as warm as honey, yet they glinted with a dark lust that she had no power to resist.

"Ask me, Helen..." he urged. She knew what he wanted her to say.

"Please..." she whispered, not able to ask for more as she leaned in to kiss him. His fingers on her thigh slid higher as their lips met. His hand on her back pulled her closer, their knees touching. His lips caressed hers in the faintest echo of a kiss before he drew back.

"Not here... Come with me." He pulled her off the loveseat and back into the hall.

They ascended the stairs together and Helen couldn't help but sense the inevitability of her situation. Tonight Gareth would possess her, body and soul, and she would not resist. She had to know how deep her passion for him ran. It was a dangerous question, but one that needed an answer.

She slowed as they passed her bedchamber, but he kept walking. At the end of the hall, he opened a door to another bedroom. It had to be his. There was an expansive four-poster bed, much bigger than the one she'd slept in. The sunlight weakened as dusk came in through the gauzy white curtains outlining the large windows. Gareth locked the door and faced her.

As he came towards her, the trembling started somewhere in her chest and spread throughout her body. He took her hands, holding them for a few seconds and absorbing the trembling before guiding her hands to his waist. Tentatively, she helped him pull his shirt out from his pants and up over his head. The flex of muscles and the broad expanse of sun-kissed skin made her a little dizzy. She had never been this close to an unclothed man. She was in turn nervous and excited.

She felt better, being in control of him as he undressed. He raised her hands to his lips, kissing them before he put them on his chest. For a long moment, she let the heat of his chest warm her, feeling the steady beat of his heart. His fingers curled around her wrists, keeping her close and anchoring her to him. She grew braver, exploring the smooth masculine skin. His hands followed hers at first, as though silently guiding her, showing her where her touch pleased him the most. Every time she swept her fingers around his flat nipples, across his throat, or down the slope of his abdomen, his lashes would lower and his lips would part with a faint panting breath.

She was so consumed with stroking his chest and watching his muscles ripple that she barely noticed his hands unlacing the back of her gown until it dropped to the floor at her feet in a whisper of fabric against flesh. He tugged gently at the several layers of petticoats and lifted her out from the mass of undergarments.

She remained quiet, heart racing, as he loosened her stays and those, too, fell to her ankles. When she was down to nothing but a chemise, Gareth wrapped his hands around her waist, picked her up, and set her on the edge of the bed. His hands slid her stockings off and moved her chemise up inch by agonizing inch.

She started trembling again and found the courage to speak his name. "Gareth..."

He froze when she spoke, his bright eyes shining in the gloom. "Yes?" he whispered.

"I'm nervous..." she confessed as his hands started moving again, baring her legs completely.

"I would never harm you. How can I convince you?" He moved slowly between her legs so that he stood against the bed's edge, their hips close but not quite touching.

"Kiss me. I forget everything else when you kiss me."

"Your wish is my command," he murmured, then delved deeply into her mouth with his tongue.

Her fear slowly receded in the wake of his consuming kisses. She didn't notice that he had pushed her back and removed his breeches. His mouth never left hers. He eased himself down on top of her, and she wrapped her legs around him, molding herself to his shape. His kisses became feverous and distracting until his length started to slide into her wet, swollen flesh. Helen dug her nails into his back, the spasm of pain shocking her as something tore deep inside her. She wanted to cry, but Gareth's kisses softened, and she relaxed. The pain lessened and finally faded. A tension replaced it, a desperate ache that she'd never felt before. He needed to move harder, faster, to ease the need.

"Are you all right?" he asked, holding still above her.

She nodded jerkily. "Yes. It doesn't hurt as much now."

Helen moved beneath him, raising her hips, completely wanton and crazed with desire. His hands slid the chemise up and off her body, barely missing a second of her kisses. Her breasts pressed against his smooth, hard chest, and a tremulous sigh escaped her lips as he settled deeper into her body. It felt right, this union in the darkness and the rushed thrill of their hips meeting and withdrawing, the touch of limbs, and the caress of lips in forbidden places.

Gareth grew tighter inside her, his movements harder, and she matched his pace, yearning to release the tension coiling in her own body. They came together, his eyes locking upon hers as their passion crested like a mighty wave. He relaxed into her as a flare of heat spread deep inside her. She kissed his lips and cheek, murmuring his name over and over again like a midnight prayer as pure joy shook her entire body. He opened his mouth as though to speak but seemed to change his mind and kissed her again. When he regained his strength, he eased off her but pulled her to him, cradling her in his arms. Even with the press of his warm body against hers, she shivered.

"Are you hurting?" He stroked her arm, trailing his fingertips down over one of her breasts. Her skin burned as he teased the soft curve of her hip and let his hand rest on her thigh.

"No... I'm just a little cold," she whispered back.

He chuckled and moved away, pulling the covers back onto the bed so they could slide between the sheets. "Better?"

"Much better." She rolled onto her side to face him. He was a dark silhouette against the moonlit windows behind him. Gareth brushed a lock of her hair back from her face, his thumb tracing her lower lip. She felt safe, content... Nothing in the world could ever harm her, not so long as he touched her, held her close. Helen drifted to sleep beneath his protective embrace.

GARETH WATCHED HER EYELIDS FALL SHUT AND LISTENED TO HER soft steady breath as she drifted to sleep. She was so trusting, to give him her virginity, knowing it should have gone to the man she would have married. It was a gift, one he vowed to cherish. He smoothed a hand down the flair of her full hips, perfect for him to hold. It felt incredible to hold a woman in his arms, and not just any woman, but Helen. There was something irresistible about her that kept drawing him in like a moth to a flame.

At last he had found the contentment he'd been robbed of. The years he'd wasted looking in all the wrong places. One simple night with Helen had cleansed his heart. In her little sighs, shivers, and kisses, he'd been reborn. It reminded him of his time with Clarissa. Theirs had been a love match—a powerful one. They had played and romped about as children, quarreled as lovers, and united as man and wife.

Apart from his best friend, Ambrose Worthing, there had been no other person in his life he had trusted himself to love. But with Helen, he could feel that giddy rush of first passion and knew it could all too easily strengthen into deep love. It was dangerous to care for her as he did, but there could be no denying his feelings.

Could he marry her? He'd believed it wasn't possible, but he had ruined her, despite knowing he should not have touched her or kissed her. He'd gone and taken everything she could give and still wanted more. Gareth started to smile at the idea of marriage, but his smile wilted. He did not deserve Helen. She ought to have been courted properly by some strapping young lad who would write sonnets about her cornflower blue eyes and the tinkling bell of her laugh.

What could he offer her? An empty home, a wasted life, and a husband who was afraid to love? A woman often believed she loved the first man who showed her passion, but she might not love him. Could she come to love him in time? If he were to convince her to wed him? Would it be enough? If they married, would their union withstand being born as a ruthless transaction? Her virtue for his honor?

ABOUT THE AUTHOR

Lauren Smith is an Oklahoma attorney by day, author by night who pens adventurous and edgy romance stories by the light of her smart phone flashlight app. She knew she was destined to be a romance writer when she attempted to re-write the entire *Titanic* movie just to save Jack from drowning. Connecting with readers by writing emotionally moving, realistic and sexy romances no matter what time period is her passion. She's won multiple awards in several romance subgenres including: New England Reader's Choice Awards, Greater Detroit BookSeller's Best

Awards, and a Semi-Finalist award for the Mary Wollstonecraft Shelley Award.

To Connect with Lauren, visit her at:

www.laurensmithbooks.com
lauren@laurensmithbooks.com

CPSIA information can be obtained
at www.ICGtesting.com
Printed in the USA
LVHW07s2321190218
567131LV00025BA/398/P